"What have you done with my bodyguard?"

His scorn was not promising. "Your security is sadly lacking, Madam President. The most inept criminal could get to you with little trouble. And that's a problem."

"My security is fine...."

He took another step closer, his hands sliding free of his pockets like a tiger unsheathing his claws. He was Bollywood handsome, with his tanned skin and honey-gold eyes, and she found herself thinking again of tigers. Sleek, gorgeous, deadly.

Instinctively she backed away. "Step aside and let me leave."

His sensual lips parted in a mocking smile. Her heart stuttered, then tripped forward again. *Too handsome and flashy. Too, too dangerous.* She had no use for men like this. No use for *any* man, she silently corrected. Not for a long time now. Not since she'd realized there were consequences to be faced.

"I'm afraid I can't do that just yet, Madam President."

All about the author…
Lynn Raye Harris

LYNN RAYE HARRIS read her first Harlequin romance when her grandmother carted home a box from a yard sale. She didn't know she wanted to be a writer then, but she definitely knew she wanted to marry a sheikh or a prince and live the glamorous life she read about in the pages. Instead, she married a military man and moved around the world. She's been inside the Kremlin, hiked up a Korean mountain, floated on a gondola in Venice and stood inside volcanoes at opposite ends of the world.

These days Lynn lives in north Alabama with her handsome husband and two crazy cats. When she's not writing, she loves to read, shop for antiques, cook gourmet meals and try new wines. She is also an avowed shoeaholic and thinks there's nothing better than a new pair of high heels.

Lynn was a finalist in the 2008 Romance Writers of America's Golden Heart contest, and she is the winner of the Harlequin Presents Instant Seduction contest. She loves a hot hero, a heroine with attitude, and a happy ending. Writing passionate stories for Harlequin Books is a dream come true. You can visit her at www.lynnrayeharris.com.

Other titles by Lynn Raye Harris available in eBook

Harlequin Presents®

Lynn Raye Harris

CAPTIVE BUT FORBIDDEN

Harlequin®

TORONTO NEW YORK LONDON
AMSTERDAM PARIS SYDNEY HAMBURG
STOCKHOLM ATHENS TOKYO MILAN MADRID
PRAGUE WARSAW BUDAPEST AUCKLAND

Recycling programs
for this product may
not exist in your area.

ISBN-13: 978-0-373-23844-6

CAPTIVE BUT FORBIDDEN

FIRST NORTH AMERICAN PUBLICATION 2012

CAPTIVE BUT FORBIDDEN

CHAPTER ONE

Late November, London

THE President of Aliz was hiding in the ladies' room.

Veronica St. Germaine lifted her head, frowning at her reflection in the mirror. She really should go back out there, but she was tired of smiling, tired of shaking hands and making small talk, tired of feeling desperate and overwhelmed and so very out of her element.

Yet she knew she had a job to do.

For Aliz. Her people needed her, and she would not fail them. They'd entrusted her with their welfare and she would not return empty-handed.

She couldn't.

Momentarily, she would go back to the hotel ballroom and paste on a smile. Just as soon as she regained her center of calm.

She couldn't quite say what had triggered her

need to escape. Perhaps it was the huge crush of curious faces, the suggestive looks from some of the men, or even the knowledge that she was surrounded by men in black suits who would dog her every step for the next two years of her life.

That was what she hated most of all—the loss of her autonomy. In truth, it sparked unpleasant associations she would rather forget. Until the age of eighteen, her life had been so tightly regimented that she'd not had even a single friend.

Veronica took a deep breath and pulled a lipstick tube from her purse. Another moment, and then she had to return to the elegant party.

She'd been traveling for the past two weeks, trying to drum up investment in her country. It wasn't an easy prospect. Aliz was beautiful, with beaches and coastline and balmy breezes, but it was also poor after so many years of mismanagement. Investors wanted to know that if they poured money into the country, it wouldn't be in vain.

She was here to convince them Aliz was a good bet.

And it was much more difficult than she'd anticipated. In so many ways, she wasn't prepared for this job. She'd said no to running for office, but Paul Durand—an old friend of her father's—had convinced her she was the person who could make everything right again.

She'd laughed at the idea—who was she to be president of a nation? She was famous in Aliz, but she was infamous the world over. There was a difference between the two, but Paul hadn't listened.

He'd spoken with such passion, such conviction. And he'd convinced her she was the one person who could do the most good for Aliz. Her notoriety, far from being undesirable, was an asset in the public arena.

She reminded herself of that now. She'd done many things wrong in her life, but she would do this right. Aliz needed her. And she was not the same person she'd been when she'd fled her father's house ten years ago.

Then, she'd been headstrong, selfish and a touch naive.

She'd been looking for adventure, and she'd done everything to excess once she'd escaped her father's control. It had been inevitable that she would become a bad girl, a diva, a spoiled debutante. Some would even include wanton seductress on that list, but all she would say was that she'd allowed herself the freedom to take lovers when it had suited her.

A dart of pain lodged beneath her breastbone.

Her last relationship had not ended so well—though it wasn't the man who'd caused the pain that even now threatened to consume her.

If she stopped fighting for even a moment, the pain would win. Because it was her fault it had happened. Her fault the tiny life growing inside her had never had a chance.

She'd always felt impervious, as if no one could hurt her because she refused to let them, but she'd learned there were many kinds of hurt. Some hurts snuck up on you like a scorpion in the night and left you gasping and aching and wondering how you'd never known it could happen to you.

Veronica swiped a hand beneath her eyes.

Not now. She would not dwell on it now.

The lights flickered overhead. It had been snowing heavily for hours. Perhaps the power would go out after all. She resolutely sucked in a breath and bent toward the mirror to remove all traces of tears from the corners of her eyes. Then she stood and smoothed a hand down her gown.

Her pity party was finished; it was time to return to the ballroom before the power went out and she was left in the dark alone.

Veronica bit back a cry as the door to the ladies' room suddenly swung inward. No one should have gotten past the bodyguard stationed outside.

But the intruder was a man, dressed in an all-too-familiar black suit.

She pivoted angrily. This was too much. She would not have her private moments intruded on by her security staff.

Except this man was not her guard, nor was he wearing the typical black suit of one of her people.

"Who are you?" she blurted, her heart beginning to hammer in her throat as she faced him.

The man was tall and clad in a tuxedo that appeared to be custom-fitted. The fabric looked expensive, with a hint of shine that came from how tightly the cloth was woven. His dark hair curled over his collar, his golden skin so exotic and beautiful.

She'd seen this man by the bar, talking to her old friend Brady Thompson. She relaxed infinitesimally. If he knew Brady...

"I am Rajesh Vala."

The name meant nothing to her.

His hands were shoved casually into the pockets of his trousers. The door swung shut behind him, and then it was just the two of them in the small anterior suite of the powder room. Mirrors lined three walls, giving her the impression there was more than one man in the room with her.

She swallowed, the pulse in her neck tapping a rhythm he surely could see.

He said nothing, as if he were waiting for her to speak. But she couldn't. She could only stare. He was Bollywood-handsome, with his tanned skin and honey-gold eyes, and she found herself thinking of tigers. Sleek, gorgeous, deadly.

Her heart kicked up again and she found her voice. "What have you done with my bodyguard?"

His scorn was not promising. "Your security is sadly lacking, Madam President. The most inept criminal could get to you with little trouble. And that's a problem."

"My security is fine—"

He took another step closer, his hands sliding free of his pockets like an animal unsheathing its claws. Instinctively, she backed away, her bottom hitting the ledge she'd rested her purse on only a few moments ago.

He held up his hands. "I'm not here to hurt you."

"Then step aside and let me leave."

His sensual lips parted in a mocking smile. Her heart stuttered, then tripped forward again. *Too handsome and flashy. Too, too dangerous.*

LYNN RAYE HARRIS 13

She had no use for men like this. No use for *any* man, she silently corrected, not for a long time now. Not since she'd realized there were consequences to be paid.

"I'm afraid I can't do that just yet, Madam President."

"I beg your pardon?" Veronica said, as coldly as she was able to. She'd learned, over the years, to brazen her way through when necessary. Sometimes all it took was the perception of authority to actually imbue authority. "That is not your decision to make."

Again the concentrated power of the leashed tiger reflected in his eyes. "Ah, but it is."

A chill rippled down her spine like the beginnings of an avalanche. Understanding unfolded within. She'd seen this man with Brady, but she had no idea who he really was.

What he was capable of.

Why he was here, now.

Her pulse throbbed even faster. "What have you done to my bodyguard? If you've hurt him…"

His head tilted. "He is special to you?"

Veronica clasped her tiny purse in both hands, holding it in front of her body like a shield. A very inadequate shield. A sudden, overwhelming urge to walk over and wipe the superior look off this man's face rolled through her. She would not act upon it, however.

"He is my countryman, and he's in my employ. Yes, I care about him."

"I see. Admirable of you, Madam President. But tell me, why are you not so careful with your own person?"

Veronica gave her head a little shake. She almost felt as if she'd been drinking, when in fact she'd had nothing stronger than sparkling water, so completely did this man befuddle her senses. "I beg your pardon?"

"Once more with the begging? I'm surprised. I understood that you were far more fierce than this."

A current of anger spiked in her belly. "I'm afraid you have me at a disadvantage, Mr. Vala. You seem to know so much about me, and I know nothing of you. Other than I saw you talking with Brady Thompson in the bar."

"So you *were* paying attention."

Veronica ground her teeth in frustration. "I would appreciate it very much if you could stop talking to me like I'm a two-year-old and tell me what you want."

Rajesh Vala laughed. The sound startled her. It was rich, deep. Sexy. It curled around her, slid through her. Disconcerted her.

"Very good, Veronica. No wonder they elected you. You project competence, regardless of whether or not it's true."

She refused to rise to the bait, though a worm of hurt burrowed through her composure. But what did she expect? She'd spent years being the kind of person no one would ever take seriously.

"If you truly know Brady, then you'll know you aren't impressing me at the moment. What is the purpose of the exercise, Mr. Vala?"

His golden eyes sparkled. Those sensual lips twitched. She found herself focusing on them, thinking how they would feel pressed against her own.

The thought shocked her. She hadn't felt the slightest hint of interest or attraction for any man in over a year. She simply wasn't ready for it.

To say this was an inconvenient time for those feelings to return was an understatement.

"No purpose, other than to see how good your security is. It isn't." He leaned against the wall, arms folded across his chest. It was such a casual pose.

But it was deceptive. She had the impression that he wasn't relaxed at all. That he could spring into action at any second. Could strike without warning.

Like a scorpion in the night.

"The guard?" she demanded again.

"He's fine. He might even be achieving his own personal Shangri-la right about now. Depending on his staying power, of course."

She felt her face redden and she glanced away. Since when did she blush over innuendo? She was Veronica St. Germaine, notorious trendsetter. She'd once attended a party in Saint-Tropez wearing a dress that had been airbrushed onto her body. She'd literally been naked, other than the paint.

And this man made her blush?

"He was quite easily distracted, by the way. The charms of lovely Tammy, an Irish lass from Cork, were too much to resist, it seems."

"You're despicable."

"No. I'm thorough. And quite adept at staying."

Her ears were on fire. She was no longer certain what they were talking about. Security? Sex? Her mind was opting for sex and her body was reacting to the suggestion.

It'd been too long since she'd had sex. That had to be the only reason he could make her flush like an innocent virgin.

"I can't imagine that Brady approves of your methods," she said coolly. It was the first thing she could think of to say that might bring the conversation back from the brink.

"Not always. But he knows I'm the best."

She wanted to sit. The heat was going to her head, making her feel faint. Or perhaps her dress was too tight. Whatever the case, she was moist with perspiration. She sank onto the bench, uncaring what he might think, and clasped her hands in her lap. Though what she really wanted to do was grab one of the fluffy white towels stacked on one corner of the vanity and dab her forehead with it.

"The best, Mr. Vala?" A sudden thought occurred to her. Brady had told her just this morning that she was too wound up—but he wouldn't hire a gigolo to relax her, would he? A gigolo who outfoxed her bodyguard and caught her in the ladies' room? A bubble of laughter escaped before she could stop it.

God, it was ridiculous. And maybe, just maybe, Brady truly was that crazy.

"I am a…security consultant," the man said, watching her curiously.

Did he think she would pat the bench and suggest they get cozy together? Was Brady so insane as to think she had bodyguard fantasies? That a handsome, too-sexy tiger in a tuxedo could rock her world in the ladies' powder room of an expensive hotel and she'd suddenly be re-laxed and ready to face the challenges await-ing her?

Once, no doubt, that would have been true. But she was a different person now. She had to be.

She found the strength to stand again. "I'm not in the mood, Mr. Vala, but I thank you for the diversion. If you could get out of my way, I'll say good-night now and return to the ballroom."

His brows drew down. She had the feeling she'd insulted him somehow.

"Perhaps you didn't hear what I said," he re-plied, taking a step toward her.

"Oh, I heard you. And I'm not sure what you and Brady cooked up between you, but I'm not that desperate. Or that stupid."

He stood so close now. So close that if she reached out, her fingertips could slide down the sleek fabric of his lapel.

His scent stole to her. Sharp and clear, like rain and warm spices. Like a sultry Indian night.

The lights dimmed for a long moment before brightening again. The tiger didn't move, his gaze never leaving her face. She felt trapped—and safe, paradoxically.

"The power will probably go out," he said.

"We should get you back to your room. It is the safest place."

"The safest place for what?" she asked, her voice little more than a cracking whisper, as her imagination ran wild and her skin grew hot and prickly.

Again, he looked at her curiously. "For you, Madam President."

Cobras. They had cobras in India. Cobras that mesmerized their prey before striking. Was he less of a tiger and more of a cobra? Was she mesmerized? Was that why she felt so languid and warm, why she wanted to close her eyes and lean into him? Why she wanted to take what she thought he was offering and then pretend it had never happened?

Deliberately, she took a step back, breaking the spell. This was insane. And she had to put an end to it. There was too much at stake.

"I'm sure you're quite good, but I've a duty to perform and no time for casual sex on the bathroom counter. Please tell Brady I was happily satisfied, if that's what you need to do to get paid. I'll find my own way back to my room."

He stared at for her a long moment—and then he threw back his head, a sharp bark of laughter springing from his throat. She was so startled she couldn't move. And then she felt the bite of heat flooding her again. A different kind of bite this time.

"This is definitely a first," he said, the humor evident on his handsome face. It transformed him somehow, made him less frightening and more real. More human. "But I am not here for your, uh, satisfaction, I assure you."

For some reason, that statement made her angry. As if he'd never consider such a thing with her. As if the thought were repulsive, when men had always clamored for her attentions.

She drew herself up. "You come in here talking in innuendo and half-truths—what do you expect me to think?"

She clung to the anger because the alternative was to melt into an embarrassed puddle. He probably had a wife and ten children at home, even if he was too perfect for words and wore no wedding band.

A sudden, sharp stab of something—*pain, Veronica, pain*—pierced her chest at heart level. She knew she was not the sort of woman who inspired visions of picket fences, warm kitchens and laughing babies.

And it had never bothered her until recently, until she'd almost had her own baby.

Baby.

Funny how that word snuck up sometimes and

squeezed the breath from her chest. She closed her eyes briefly, swallowed the bile rising in her throat.

I'm sorry, sweet baby...

"Are you unwell?" he asked.

She sliced a hand through the air impatiently, shoving the pain down deep into her soul. "I'm fine."

The lights flickered again. He looked up, frowning. "We really should return to your room before the power goes out."

"*We* aren't going anywhere," she snapped.

He looked at her as if he pitied her. "That is not your choice to make."

Veronica stared at him for a moment, undecided, while anger built into a solid wall inside her. How *dare* he? How absolutely *dare* he?

Energy exploded inside her like a wave collapsing and racing toward shore, until it sent her striding forward, intending to push past him if necessary.

He anticipated her, caught her bare arm in one strong hand. The shock of skin on skin sizzled into her core, and Veronica gasped. It was too much, too many raw emotions welling to the surface all at once. She couldn't bear it, couldn't bear to be touched by him.

She twisted hard, her open hand swinging up to connect with his cheek.

She missed. At the same time, her body spun out of her control—and then she was pressed against him, her back to his front, one strong hand clasping her wrists together behind her back while the other snaked around her waist and held her tightly.

Fury welled inside her as she jerked uselessly against the bonds of his iron grip.

He was so solid, so warm and hard. It took her a moment to realize that her bottom nestled in the cradle of his hips. That his body was responding to the way she squirmed against him. If she weren't wearing heels, she wouldn't be tall enough.

But right now, she was.

Her skin was hot, so hot. She wanted to press back against him, wanted to feel his heat pass into her cold body.

The thought horrified her so much she pulled forward in his grasp, trying hard to minimize the contact between them. Her back arched, her breasts straining against her gown as if they would pop free at any moment.

"Let me go," she groaned.

"I'm here to protect you," he said, his warm breath whispering against her ear. A shudder traveled the length of her spine. She had no doubt he'd felt it.

"Protect me from what? From you?" she flung at him as the evidence of his arousal grew against her.

He managed to put a little distance between them, though not much. The loss of contact disconcerted her in ways it shouldn't. What was wrong with her?

"From yourself," he growled in her ear. "From the incompetence of your staff."

"A funny way you have of doing it," she snapped, trying so hard to concentrate on what was wrong with this picture instead of what felt right.

His touch. His breath in her ear. The scent of him. The solid feel of him standing behind her. Veronica fought for control. "I have protection, in spite of what you might think. That man will be fired immediately. Another will take his place."

"Very good, Veronica. I'd thought you would be soft on him."

"I'm never soft," she said as another tremor passed over her. His fingers began to slide slowly across her abdomen.

"Are you quite certain?" His voice was seductive and beautiful in her ear. So much in that sentence. So much she couldn't begin to speak to.

"You can let me go," she repeated.

"I'm not so sure." His fingers moved slowly, so slowly. The pressure of them against her body was light, yet she felt them as if she was naked and he was stroking her like a lover.

She closed her eyes, swallowed hard. *My God...*

The lights flickered once more....

And then snapped out, plunging them into darkness.

CHAPTER TWO

THE sudden silence was crushing. Veronica could hear his breathing, but nothing else.

"Now what?" she asked, her voice so loud to her ears. Catching at the end. Sounding husky. Needy.

For this man? A stranger to her?

It was unfathomable, and yet nothing was as it should be. Nothing had been as it should have been for months. In truth, her entire life had spun out of control and had yet to spin back.

"We wait," he said, his fingers stilling.

"For what? Don't you have a flashlight or something? For all your fine talk about being the best, you seem unprepared."

"I am definitely prepared," he growled in her ear, his breath tickling the fine hairs on her nape.

"Prove it," she said, her voice even huskier if that were possible. Dear God, what was she up to? There was no way on earth she was truly egging this man on, was there? She might find

him amazingly attractive—devastatingly so—
but she was not about to lift her gown and wrap
her legs around his body in reality.

No matter what Brady seemed to think she
was capable of. No matter what she might have
done a little over a year ago when confronted
with a man of such beauty and power as this
sexy tiger in black.

The old Veronica would have made *him* blush.

"I'm beginning to understand you," he said in
her ear. "You challenge those around you as a
way to deflect attention from yourself. And yet
you've been elected to a very public position.
Odd, is it not?"

A stone dropped inside her stomach. It was
too close to the truth. Too close to who she'd
been before she'd lost her way. "Save yourself
the trouble of trying to analyze me, Mr. Vala."

"Don't you think you should call me Raj
now?" His hand around her wrists was hot, his
skin still burning hers with his touch. Though
it was dark, she closed her eyes.

Raj. It was exotic, like him. She wanted to say
it aloud, wanted to try it on her tongue.

But she would not.

"I see no need," she said. "As soon as the
lights come back on, I don't ever intend to see
you again."

"You need me, Veronica. Whether you wish to admit it or not."

She swallowed. "I don't need anyone." She'd made sure of it over the years—and she'd only been wrong once.

His hand dropped from her waist. A moment later, she felt the tips of his fingers sliding along her spine where her dress opened, leaving a trail of fire in their wake. "Mr. Vala…"

"Raj."

"Raj," she said, giving in to his demand because she hoped it would stop the insane stroking of her skin. It did not.

She *wanted*. And yet she couldn't allow this side of her nature to surface, not now. Not ever again. The only way to protect herself from harm was to suppress her feelings. Feelings of need, of loneliness, of desire.

Human feelings.

No.

Veronica sucked in a shaky breath, fighting for control. "This isn't very professional, is it? Do security consultants usually attempt to seduce their charges?"

The torturous track of his fingers ceased. Her heart hammered in the thick darkness. She'd scored a hit, but it didn't make her feel any better. In some ways she wanted to take the words back, wanted him to continue the light stroking of her skin.

He did not. "Forgive me," he said, his tone clipped—but whether it was with anger at her or himself, she wasn't certain.

A moment later she was moving sideways, falling—but just as she was about to grab for him, about to wrap her arms around his neck so she didn't fall, he eased her down on a bench and let her go. She searched the blackness for him, but could see nothing. Panic filled her until she willed it away.

"Don't leave me here," she said, nearly choking on the words as she did so. She hated to admit weakness, hated to admit she did need him, at least for the time being.

"I'm not leaving," he replied, his voice coming from across the room. But she could hear the door easing open. He was going to leave her alone in this dark, lonely room. She would be lost, as lost as she'd been at sixteen when her father had locked her in a closet to punish her for trying to run away.

Blindly, she shot upright…and fell forward as her foot hit a nearby table.

Somehow, she managed to catch herself, but not without bending her wrist too far. She cried out as needles of pain shot through her arm.

"What are you doing?" Raj demanded.

She groped her way back onto the bench, relief flooding her as she held her wrist, sucking in deep breaths to keep from crying. "I thought you were leaving."

"I told you I wasn't." His voice sounded closer now. A second later, light illuminated the small room.

She blinked up at him. "You have a light."

"Yes."

"Why didn't you use it to begin with?"

"Because I needed to be sure no one was outside first." He bent in front of her, his dark head close as he took her arm in his hands and probed her wrist. She didn't bother to ask how he knew she'd hurt herself. Veronica hissed as he found the tender spot. "It's just a light sprain," he said.

Then he stood and the light blinked out again.

"Why do we have to sit here?" she asked. "Why can't we use your light and go to my room?"

"So now you want my help," he said softly, almost teasingly.

"You have the light," she replied, as if it were the most logical thing in the world to say.

She felt movement, felt a solid form settle on the bench beside her. He reached for her arm, finding it so surely that she swore he must have a cat's night vision.

His fingers danced over the skin of her wrist, his thumbs pressing in deeply, making her gasp—and yet it felt good, as if he were easing the sprain out of her by touch alone.

"This is what we are going to do," he said. "We're going to spend the next twenty minutes here, while pandemonium reigns in the hotel, and hope the lights come back on. If they don't, we're going to your room."

She hated being told what to do, and yet she'd tacitly agreed to it when she'd panicked over being alone in the dark. "Did Brady hire you?"

His soft snort was confusing. "In a manner of speaking. I've done work for him in the past. Protecting his celebrity clients."

She had to bite back a moan as his fingers worked their magic on her. "I appreciate your diligence, Mr. Vala, but Brady should have known better."

"He cares about you."

"I know," she said softly. Brady was a true friend. She knew he'd always wanted to be more than that, but she'd never felt the same in return. In spite of it, their friendship flourished. Brady was a good man, the kind of man she *should* have been interested in. Life would have been a whole lot easier if she had been.

The pressure of Raj's fingers was perfect, rhythmic. Why did she always want the kind of men who were terrible for her? Men like this one, handsome and dangerous and incapable of seeing past the facade of her outward appearance to what lay beneath?

It was her fault they could not. She'd spent so many years building a wall, becoming someone interesting and compelling and, yes, even shocking, that she no longer knew how to be herself with a man. She had no idea if the real Veronica was even worth the trouble.

And she wasn't planning to try and find out.

Raj's voice startled her. "After what happened tonight, do you still trust your staff?"

A chill slithered down her spine. That was something she hadn't wanted to think about. Because how could she admit that she didn't know? That she was out of her depth and uncertain where to turn?

She thought of the letter she'd gotten that morning, and shivered. It had been so simple, one word in cut-out letters: *slut.* It had been nothing, really. The work of a former rival. Who else would go to the trouble?

But the one question she'd kept asking herself

today was how had the letter penetrated her security and found its way onto her breakfast tray?

She'd interrogated her secretary. The guard on duty. The maid. The porter. No one seemed to know.

Then, in a moment of weakness, she'd told Brady about it. She regretted that now, as it was surely the impetus for him to call this man.

"Yes, I trust them," she said, because she could say nothing else. Was she supposed to run scared over a simple letter? Her bodyguard abandoning his post tonight was an unrelated incident. That didn't mean the rest of her staff was incompetent.

"Then you are either naive or stupid, Madam President," Raj Vala said.

"I am neither one," she replied, bristling not only at the way he'd pronounced her incompetent, but also at the condescending tone he'd used to say the last two words. As if he didn't think her worthy.

She might not be, but it wasn't his place to say so. He was not Alizean. "Not everything is as straightforward as you might think. There are many options to be considered."

His thumbs worked magic. Tingles of sensation streaked up her arm, over her scalp. Down into her core. She couldn't stop the little moan that escaped her.

Damn him. And damn her reawakened senses.

Wrong time. Wrong place. Wrong man.

It was the situation, she told herself, the fact she now found herself alone with a dynamic, sexy stranger who touched her as if he had a right. Because she'd allowed no man to get close to her since the miscarriage, she was now suffering from sensory overload.

"Would you like me to tell you the best option?" he asked.

"Do I have a choice?" she snapped.

"You always have a choice," he replied evenly. "Except in instances where your immediate safety might be at stake."

She wanted to tell him to go to hell. Who was he to walk in here and try to take over this aspect of her new life as if he had a right?

But he kept rubbing, soothing her sore wrist, and she didn't say a word because she selfishly didn't want him to stop.

A minute later, the fingers of one hand slid up her arm, over her jaw, her chin, across her lips. She didn't know why she allowed it—

No, that wasn't quite true. She allowed it because it felt shockingly perfect to let him touch her. He made her feel normal, and that was something she hadn't expected to feel ever again. It felt surprisingly good to be touched after all this time.

She trembled at the featherlight stroking of his finger across her mouth, and she bit down on her lip to keep from nibbling him in return.

Oh, he was good. Good enough that she began to wonder if he hadn't missed his calling in life. Gigolo seemed a perfectly acceptable occupation for a man with his skill set.

"Then tell me this option," she stated, hoping she sounded businesslike and cool as she dragged her attention back from the summit. "Let's see how good you are."

His fingers slid along her jaw now, so light, so erotic. His soft laugh was a sensual purr in his throat, and she knew she'd made a mistake. A dreadful, heart-pounding mistake.

"It's quite simple. You need to acquire a lover, Madam President." His voice was so sexy, so mesmerizing, his slight British accent combined with another she couldn't quite place.

Everything inside her stilled. Her stomach clenched painfully. *Of course.*

He might be here to help her, but he wasn't above helping himself, either. Men like him made her sick. Always wanting something in return. Brady might truly care, but this man did not.

"It's out of the question," she said, her voice tight. "I don't want to hear another word of this—"

"Ah, but you will listen. Because you're smart, Veronica." His fingers continued their damning track across her skin. She felt his presence in the dark as a solid wall of heat, and she tilted her head back, sensing somehow that he loomed over her, that his mouth was only inches from hers.

She should pull away, and yet she couldn't seem to do it. "Flattery will get you nowhere."

"Why deny the truth? You know it as well as I do."

Heat suffused her from the inside out. Somehow she managed to scoot backward on the bench, to put distance between them. Was she that transparent? "I have no idea what you're talking about."

But she did. Because he touched her so lightly, so expertly, that her body was tightening like a bowstring.

There was definitely something there, something between them…something that would combust if she let it. Part of her desperately wanted to let it…

"Yes, you do," he said softly. His tone was that of a lover.

Did he feel it, too?

"Maybe…" she breathed.

But his next words shattered that illusion.

"Your presidency is too new, Aliz is in turmoil and you aren't safe."

Every word was like a blow. Embarrassment flooded her in bright, white-hot waves. She'd been preoccupied with the way he made her feel when he touched her, and he was nothing but business. Damn him for making her forget, even for a moment.

"Those things are none of your concern," she said evenly, thankful he couldn't see her flushed face. Thankful there was no light to give her away. "Nothing you can do will fix it overnight."

"This isn't a game, Veronica. You can't quit this party when it no longer amuses you." Raj heard her draw in a breath. He'd probably insulted her, but he didn't give a damn.

Because Veronica St. Germaine was precisely the sort of woman he had no sympathy for.

She was a slave to her passions, her wants, her desires. She was the worst kind of person to be entrusted with the welfare of a puppy, let alone a nation—yet here she was.

And here he was, damn Brady to hell. Raj

hadn't wanted to do this job, but Brady had begged him.

For old time's sake. And since Raj owed at least a measure of his success to Brady's faith in him when he'd been fresh out of the military and working his first security job so many years ago, he couldn't say no.

So now he was sitting in the dark with a too-sexy, spoiled society princess and arguing over whether or not she needed his help.

He should just kiss her and put the matter to rest. He wasn't unaware of her response to him. He also wasn't unaware of her reputation as a woman who pursued her appetites relentlessly, be they clothes, shoes, fast cars or men.

And at least one part of his anatomy didn't mind the prospect of being an object of her desire.

Not that he would allow himself to go down that road.

It'd been a long time since he'd personally guarded anyone, but he had never allowed himself to get involved with a client. It angered him immensely that he'd nearly violated that creed with her.

He didn't know why he'd allowed himself to succumb to the temptation to stroke his fingers along the creamy skin of her exposed back. She was not the kind of woman he would ever get involved with. It wasn't that she wasn't desirable—she definitely was—but she was self-centered and destructive. Poisonous.

"I know this isn't a game!" she barked. "Do you really think I don't?"

He'd heard those words before. Or ones very like them anyway. He knew all about people who had no control over their impulses. People who claimed to want to conquer their addictions, but inevitably slid back into them when life got too hard or too boring or too hopeless.

He had no sympathy for her. She'd taken on this task, and she deserved no pity if it was turning out to be too difficult. After all, her people would get none if she faltered. "It's a big responsibility you've accepted. Not quite your usual thing, is it?"

He could feel the fury rolling from her in waves.

"You know nothing about me, Mr. Vala. I'd appreciate it if you'd keep your pop psychology to yourself."

She was cool, this woman. And blazing hot on the inside. He was beginning to understand the public fascination with her.

He'd made sure to have his people prepare a dossier on her before he'd ever come to the hotel tonight. He hadn't read the entire thing during the limo ride over, but he'd skimmed enough to get an idea.

A dilettante in the worlds of fashion, music and television, she'd designed a line of clothing, recorded a hit album and had her own late-night talk show for a brief time in America.

She'd been a darling of the tabloids. Her face and figure were splashed on more magazine covers worldwide than were the royals. It was astounding.

Until about a year ago, she'd regularly appeared. Then she'd dropped out of sight. Working on a new project, her spokesperson had said at the time, though the speculation had been that she was nursing a broken heart after a failed affair.

When she'd emerged from hiding four months later, she'd been relegated to a small blurb on the pages she'd once dominated. It had been shortly afterward that she'd declared her candidacy for president.

It wasn't difficult to figure out why she'd done so, because suddenly she was back on top, a darling of the media once more.

He understood where that kind of need for attention came from, but he had no patience for it.

People like her destroyed those foolish enough to get close to them.

Or those who had no choice—like children.

More than once he'd watched his mother spiral into the depths of her selfish need for attention, unable to stop her. Unable to prevent the crash. He'd survived that life, but he certainly hadn't come away unscathed.

"A lover could get close to you without suspicion," he said. "It would be a way to provide extra security without anyone on your staff questioning the addition."

"You aren't listening to me, are you? I don't like you, and I can't take a lover. Even a false one."

He didn't bother to point out that she did like him. That she'd been sending him signals from the moment he'd entered the room. Frustration hammered into him. Why was he arguing with her? He'd done what he'd promised Brady he would do. He'd tried to help. Now he could take her back to her suite and leave her there in good conscience.

Except it wasn't in his nature to give up so easily, especially when he believed she truly was in danger. Her country was in turmoil, and it was well-known that the previous president hadn't been too happy with the outcome of the election. Aliz was a democracy, but only just. And Monsieur Brun had been in power for twelve years before he'd lost to this woman who had no political experience whatsoever.

Disgruntled loser was an understatement.

"You need protection, Veronica. That threat should never have gotten through the layers surrounding you. It will escalate, believe me."

He could feel her stiffen beside him. "There's been no threat."

"That's not what Brady says."

Her breath hissed out. "I *knew* it. It was *one* word, made of newspaper letters and glued to a piece of paper. That's hardly a threat!"

Every instinct he had told him otherwise. It was an ugly word, the kind of word that was filled with hate and derision. Spoken in anger was one thing. Deliberately pasted together and sent? "Did you keep the letter?"

"I threw it away."

He'd expected as much, though it would have been better if she had not. "Has it happened before?"

"Before I was president?"

"Precisely."

She let out a frustrated breath. "No. But that doesn't mean anything. Everyone has enemies."

"But not everyone is the president of a nation. You have to take every anomaly, no matter how small, as a legitimate threat. You have no choice now."

"I realize that." Her voice was ice.

"Then you must also realize that we wouldn't actually be lovers," he said, as much to himself as to her. "That's not why I'm here."

A shame, really. She was an extraordinarily sensual woman. He'd watched her work the room from his position at the bar earlier. She'd slain men with her smile, with the high, firm breasts that jutted into the fabric of the purple dress she wore. With the long, beautiful legs he'd glimpsed through the slit in the fabric when she walked.

Her platinum-blond hair was piled onto her head, and her dress dipped low in the back, revealing smooth, touchable skin. Men had tripped over their tongues as they'd gathered around her. He'd watched it all with disdain.

Until he'd gotten close to her. His visceral reaction had been strong, his body hardening painfully. It was nothing he couldn't handle. He was accustomed to want, to deprivation and pain. The military had made sure of it. Denying himself pleasure, no matter how much he might want it, was easily done.

"Even the appearance of it would be too

much," she replied, her words crisp and lovely in the French accent of her homeland. "I am the president. I have an image to maintain."

"You're a single woman, Veronica. You're allowed to date. And Aliz's is not the sort of culture that would take you to task for it."

"Aliz has had one crisis after another. They need a president who is focused on their welfare, not on her personal life."

He found the words ironic coming from her, but he allowed it to pass without comment.

"They also elected you because you are glamorous and exotic to them. You've achieved fame on the world stage, and they are proud of you. If you become simply another staid politician, you will disappoint them. They want you to fix things, but they also want you to be the Veronica St. Germaine they know and love."

"You can't know that," she said angrily. "You are saying whatever you think will further your personal agenda."

A current of annoyance rippled through him, only partly because it was true. "My personal agenda? I'm doing you a favor, Madam President, in trying to protect your lovely behind."

"How dare you suggest I should be grateful when you keep trying to give me something I don't want?"

What she needed was a hard dose of reality.

He grasped her shoulders, pulled her closer to him. He did it for effect, not because he wanted to kiss her. Not because he'd been dying to kiss her from the moment she'd turned to him when he'd entered this room.

Never because of that.

Her palms came up, pressed against his chest. "What are you doing?" She sounded breathless. Not scared, not angry. Breathless. Anticipating. Wanting.

If he were a weaker man, she would be the ruin of all his fine control.

"We're alone and you're at my mercy," he said, making sure his voice was harsh rather than se-ductive. "If I'd come to harm you, no one would stop me."

"I'm not helpless," she replied. "I took a self-defense course."

Raj laughed. He couldn't help it. Self-defense was good. Everyone should take a self-defense class. And yet...

"There are people against whom your aver-age self-defense techniques don't work. Because those techniques rely on surprise, and some peo-ple cannot be surprised. Some people are trained killers, Veronica."

Like he was, he silently added. Six years in

the Special Forces had taught him that much and more.

He felt the shiver go through her body. The idea was reprehensible to her. As well it should be.

"Everything you say is for one purpose," she said, her breath soft against his face.

It wouldn't take much to claim her lips. To plunder them with his own and taste their sweetness.

"But you and Brady have got it all wrong. No one is out to harm me."

His grip on her tightened. "Are you willing to bet your life on that?"

CHAPTER THREE

VERONICA'S pulse skipped and bobbed like a white-water raft sailing toward a massive waterfall. But whether it was his insistence she was in danger or how closely he now held her, she couldn't be sure.

He gripped her so tightly that she could feel the strength of the leashed power in him. A shiver skimmed over her. He'd scared her with his talk of danger—but she wouldn't let him know it.

His hands splayed over her back. She could feel his breath on her face. She thought he might kiss her just to prove his mastery—and part of her longed for it.

Another part wanted to run as far and as fast away from this man as she could get. For whatever reason, he affected her. She'd thought herself immune to men after Andre—handsome, flashy, selfish Andre—but Raj was proving her wrong on that count.

She'd made the right decision when she'd told him she didn't need his help. No way on this earth was she allowing him to pretend to be her lover. One way or another, it would be disastrous.

She strained in the dark to hear him, to feel him, to guess his intent. His breath was on her lips. If she tilted her head, would their mouths touch? She told herself not to do it, and yet her head moved anyway.

Abruptly, he released her.

"Come," he said. "It's time to take you back to your room."

The light flashed on again, and she realized it was coming from his cell phone. His handsome face was in shadow, but she could see the gleam of his eyes as he stood and held out a hand to her.

She took it, let him pull her up, her pulse skittering wildly the instant he touched her.

"I'm not stupid," she said, feeling the need to defend herself. "If I thought there was any real danger, I'd hire you in a minute. But there isn't. The security I have can handle the day-to-day issues that arise."

The steady look he gave her said he didn't believe it for a second. "Instead of justifying it to me, perhaps you need to ask whether or not you're being honest with yourself."

Then he turned and opened the door instead of waiting for an answer. Not that she had one to give. He went through first, and then motioned her to follow. She stayed close behind him as they worked their way toward the upper floors.

The hotel was in disarray, but the staff had managed to get the emergency lights working in the main hallways and stairwells. Exit signs also provided light, though meager, and she heard scraps of conversation about the generator and its failure to provide backup power. Raj said nothing, simply led the way through the hotel until they came to her room. She was only surprised for a moment that he knew which room was hers.

Of course he knew. Brady had told him everything.

Before she could ask him how he planned to get inside with the power out and the card reader down, he had the door open.

"Behind me," he said.

It was on the tip of her tongue to thank him for his help and tell him to go, but she said nothing. Instead, she did what he told her to do. Regardless of how she felt about him—or about Brady's meddling—it was clear that Raj knew what he was doing. She felt safe, at least for the time being.

He gave her the motion to stay where she was, then went into each room of her suite in succession before returning and giving her the all clear.

Veronica let out a long sigh of relief—not that she'd expected anything to be wrong. She was just glad to be back in the privacy of her room again. She kicked off her platform stilettos, her feet sinking into the plush carpet. "Thank you for escorting me," she said. "I'd offer you a drink, but it's getting rather late. Tell Brady you tried your best. He knows how I am."

Raj fished out a lighter from somewhere and lit the candles that were sitting on the tables. She'd thought they were merely decorative and, in truth, had forgotten all about them. Then he shrugged out of his tuxedo jacket and threw it across the back of a chair.

"I'm not leaving just yet."

A hot bubble of anger popped inside her. She wanted to be alone, wanted to strip out of her gown, put on her pajamas and watch a little bit of television—assuming the power came back on—before she fell asleep. "I didn't ask you to stay."

He lifted his mobile phone and tapped a few buttons. "Until your security returns, I'm staying."

"That's really not necessary. I'll lock the door behind you."

"Forget it," he said, turning away from her to talk to someone on the phone.

Veronica sank onto the couch and folded her arms over her chest. Damn the arrogance of the man. But she already knew it was useless to order him to leave. Useless to do anything but wait.

If she were lucky, Brady would come looking for her—and then she could give them both a piece of her mind. She'd had quite enough of being told what to do lately. She had to conform to a schedule as president, had to take meetings and attend functions, had to let her day-to-day activities be far more structured than they'd been since she'd lived on her own.

But she'd agreed to do those things when she'd decided to run for office. What she hadn't agreed to do was let a dark, sexy stranger intrude on the very small slice of privacy she had remaining.

Her gaze drifted to Raj. She couldn't hear what he was saying, but he seemed engrossed in his call. He was even more golden in the candlelight than he'd been in the low lights of the powder room. So handsome. So dangerous. Like the tiger she'd first envisioned when he'd filled the small anteroom and made her aware of him on a level she wished she weren't.

A ring glinted on his right hand, a signet made of gold. She hadn't noticed that before.

His white tuxedo shirt stretched across his chest, and onyx studs winked at her in the flickering light. He reached up and loosened the stud at his neck before yanking the bow tie off and tossing it aside.

She started at the small wedge of bare skin he'd revealed. He glanced up then, straight at her, and she twisted away, cursing herself for getting caught. A moment later he ceased talking and tucked the phone into his trouser pocket.

"Was that Brady?" she asked.

"No."

Frustration knotted her stomach. Since she didn't know what else to do, she reached up and began to unpin her hair, dropping the pins onto the glass side table with a *clink, clink, clink.* Then she threaded the fingers of both hands through her hair, loosening the glossy mass.

When she stopped, Raj was watching her. He stood in the same place he had been, his gaze hard.

Her stomach flipped, her pulse humming with energy. She looked away and began to remove her jewelry.

"Have you been doing this kind of thing long?" she asked. If he insisted on staying, then the least she could do was bore him with questions. Maybe he'd decide to leave her alone after all.

"A few years."

"How exciting." She slipped off the jewelry—bracelet, necklace, rings—and dropped everything on the table with the pins. "Who's the most famous person you've ever worked for?"

"Confidential information."

She glanced up at him, her heart squeezing as she took in the masculine beauty of his face once more. "Ah, of course."

"Are you trying to interview me, Madam President?" he asked, one corner of his mouth twitching with humor.

She swallowed. Humor was not at all the effect she'd been going for. Veronica pulled her feet up beneath her and began to absently rub one instep while her blood beat in her temples, between her breasts. "Not precisely. But if we're to be stuck here together for the foreseeable future, it seems a way to pass the time."

It took her several moments to realize that the side slit in her gown had dropped open to reveal the curve of her legs. She resisted the urge to cover herself, though she suddenly wanted to do so. But she would not let him think she cared that his hot eyes skimmed her form.

"How does one get into the bodyguard business anyway?"

"You've certainly grown chatty," he observed, meeting her gaze once more. She felt heat rising in her cheeks, but she didn't look away. Then he shrugged and shoved his hands into his pockets. "I was in the military. It seemed the logical thing to do when I got out."

"Oh, I see. And do you work for a company that sends you out on these jobs?"

"In a manner of speaking," he said.

The humor was back, but this time she didn't know why.

"If this *were* a job interview," she pointed out, "I don't think I'd be inclined to hire you based on these answers. You're almost monosyllabic."

He sank onto the chair opposite, his big form sprawling comfortably—as if he belonged here, in her suite. As if *he* were the one in charge and she merely a supplicant.

She didn't like that he made her feel inconsequential simply by being in the same room.

"Fortunately, this is not an interview," he said. "You don't need me, as you've pointed out." His golden eyes speared her so that, once more, she was mesmerized. "And I don't do interviews. No one hires me. I decide if I'll help *them*."

"My, my," she said, her face growing hot for some reason. "Aren't you special?"

He leaned forward then, his gaze raking her. She only hoped he couldn't see the *tap, tap, tap* of her heart.

"That's the way *your* world works, Veronica. But not everything is a competition, and not every desire needs to be indulged. I know my worth based on what I've done in the past. I don't think I'm entitled to anything because I deserve it. I've earned it."

She didn't know whether to be outraged or embarrassed. Heat flooded her, made her want to grab a magazine off the table and fan herself. She did not. She'd made her proverbial bed, after all. It was no surprise when someone forced her to lie in it.

But she would not apologize for her life, not to this man. He could know nothing of what she'd been through. No one could.

"Until you walk a mile in someone else's shoes, perhaps it's unwise to make assumptions about them," she said, her smile as brittle as she felt.

He inclined his head a fraction. "You do that so well."

"Do what?"

"Indignation."

She thought of a million responses, discarding them each as she did so. It was no use. There was no point in trying to make this man understand. He meant nothing to her and, after tonight, their paths were unlikely to cross again.

Veronica got to her feet and stared down at him coldly. Imperiously. *Bastard.* "I believe I've had enough of this charming conversation," she said by way of dismissal. "I'm going to bed."

"If this is how you intend to handle affairs of state, Aliz is in a great deal of trouble." His words were mild, his tone nonconfrontational— but his eyes accused her, burned her.

"You are hardly an affair of state," she said, picking up one of the candles from the table, proud that she kept herself from trembling with fury as she did so. "And I'll not stay here and listen to you insult me. You've made up your mind about me. I see no need to waste my breath in pointing out the flaws in your logic."

He flicked a hand in the direction of the bedroom. "Go, then. It's far easier to run from your problems than to confront them."

"In this case," she said, "I believe it is."

Then she turned and strode away, holding her hand in front of the candle to keep it from blowing out. She closed the bedroom door firmly behind her. Fury churned and roiled in her stomach, burning like acid. Why did she let him get to her? He meant nothing to her. His opinion meant nothing.

He was no one, she reminded herself, nothing more than hired muscle. She didn't let her Alizean bodyguards irritate her half so much, so why was she allowing this man to do so?

Veronica shrugged her shoulders to ease the tension and began to get undressed.

It was a relief to shrug out of the beaded gown and into her flannel pajamas. The Christmas elves marching merrily across the fabric cheered her. She'd thought they were whimsical and cute and she'd bought them impulsively. They were warm and cozy, and she didn't regret it in the least.

Veronica went into the bathroom and washed off her makeup, then returned to the bed and jerked back the covers without removing all the fluffy pillows. Something slightly heavier than a pillow came away with the last tug and bounced down the bed, landing in the middle. She didn't remember leaving anything on the bed when she'd left the room tonight.

Curiously, she lifted the candle.

At first, she wasn't sure what the dark blob

was. But then her breath caught in her throat. She wanted to scream, but her vocal chords had seized up. Her mouth opened and closed, like a fish gulping water.

"Raj," she finally squeaked. "Raj. Raj! Raj!"

Each time she managed a little more breath, his name a little louder on every exhalation.

Until the door whipped open and he was at her side. He gripped her arms, bent his head until he was at her level. He looked concerned, intense. She realized he was speaking. Asking her what was the matter. If she were hurt.

She shook her head, turned away. She couldn't look at that…thing…again.

She knew the moment he saw it. He stiffened. Swore.

Then he hooked an arm behind her knees and swept her up against his chest. She didn't protest. She didn't want to protest. Another moment and he was striding from the room. She buried her face in his shirt and let the tears fall.

CHAPTER FOUR

His brain had switched into work mode, but his body was very aware of the woman clinging to him so tightly. Raj carried her into the living area, intending to put her on the couch and cover her with a blanket, but her arms were wrapped so tightly around his neck that he knew she wasn't about to let go.

Instead, he settled into one corner of the couch with her on his lap and started to make phone calls. Red-hot anger was a thick brew inside him. It was only a doll on her bed, but someone had gouged out its eyes and splashed what had to be red paint across its body. The alternative was too horrible to contemplate.

Someone had sent a message tonight. An ugly, brutal message if the way Veronica clung to him, her silent tears dampening the fabric of his shirt, was any indication.

No matter what he thought of her, she didn't deserve that kind of ugliness.

He let her cry, one arm firmly around her while he called in one of his security teams. He would have them sweep for any other signs of intrusion before he let Veronica stay here another night. Whether she liked it or not, he was definitely involved.

He considered having her moved to another hotel altogether, but he wasn't entirely convinced that someone on her staff wasn't behind the threats. In that case, moving would do no good. He fully intended to have them all investigated, starting immediately.

He finished the calls and laid his phone on the couch beside his leg. Veronica was curled up in his arms, her face pressed to his chest. She was wearing multicolored pajamas with elves on them—not quite what he'd expected when he'd burst into her room as she'd cried his name.

She'd scared him. He hadn't known what to expect when he'd answered her cry, though he was relieved it hadn't been worse. The doll had apparently been shoved beneath the pillows on her bed. When she'd pulled the covers free, the doll tumbled loose. He cursed himself for having missed it, but the truth was that he couldn't have known.

He would check her quarters more thoroughly in the future.

She held him tightly, but he could feel that she was beginning to be uncomfortable doing so. Her body was stiffening, her fingers opening and closing on his shirt periodically.

She didn't like being dependent on anyone. He'd guessed that about her earlier when she'd been so insistent she didn't need his help. She was proud, and used to getting her way.

A few moments more, and she began to push herself upright. He tightened his grip on her, surprised that he wanted her to stay in his arms, that she felt good there, but immediately let her move away. This changed nothing between them. She was still spoiled, still selfish and self-destructive.

He was here to do a job, nothing more.

She got to her feet, her back to him, and scrubbed her sleeve across her face. His heart pinched. But he was a professional and he would view these events dispassionately. He couldn't do his job if he were emotionally invested.

"Thank you for not saying I told you so," she said a few moments later, her back still to him. The candles flickered, and he found himself wishing she would turn around. That she would look at him.

"What was that about, Veronica?"

She shrugged. It was supposed to be a casual gesture, but it failed miserably. "I wish I knew."

He wanted to be gentle with her, yet he couldn't afford to leave anything unexamined. Her life might depend on it. "I think you do."

Her shoulders drooped. "I'm not prepared to discuss it," she said softly.

In that moment, he had to admit that he admired her more than he'd thought possible. She could have lied, could have insisted she didn't know what he was talking about. But she didn't.

"I don't know who could have done it, and that's the truth," she continued.

Raj stood and put a hand on her shoulder, squeezed. "You don't want to talk about it. I can respect that—for now. But there may come a time when you have no choice."

She turned to him then. A sharp stab of emotion pierced him at gut level. Her face was so fresh and young, so innocent. She'd removed all her makeup and stood before him with red-rimmed eyes, the tracks of her tears gleaming in the candlelight.

He wanted to pull her into his arms, tuck her head against his chest and tell her it would be okay. Instead, he kept his arms rigid at his sides.

"Thank you." She dropped her gaze away, as if she suddenly couldn't look at him. For some reason, that bothered him. She'd been so fiery earlier, so confrontational. She hadn't backed down once. This Veronica was too timid, too defeated.

He didn't like it.

Raj put a finger under her chin, forced her to look at him. Her eyes glistened, but she didn't cry. He could tell that she was finished with crying. Determined.

"Will you let me help you now?" He phrased it as a question, though as far as he was concerned there was no question.

Her throat moved. "Yes," she said, her voice uncertain, thready. She repeated it, the word stronger this time.

"A wise decision," he said.

Her expression hardened, just for a moment. "My staff can't know."

He'd already considered that. If someone in her employ *was* doing these things, it wouldn't do any good for them to know she had extra security.

"Then we're back to the original plan," he said. "Can you do it?"

Her eyes flashed. But she thrust her chin out and gave a firm nod. "If that's what it takes, yes."

He grinned at her. That's the Veronica he'd been looking for. "Then we'll begin tonight."

Her eyes dropped, boldly taking in his form. Then she met his gaze again, one eyebrow quirking. "You're a bit overdressed for the part, considering what I'm wearing."

His body went from zero to sixty in half a second. He couldn't help it, though he was thankful the room was dark enough she couldn't tell.

"We'll improvise," he told her. Because he most certainly wasn't stripping down to his silk boxers.

She wrapped her arms around herself, once more the vulnerable, helpless innocent. He reminded himself that she was neither of those things, though she was certainly frightened— and with good reason.

He put his hands on her shoulders. "You can trust me utterly, Veronica. I won't let anything happen to you."

She let out a shaky sigh. "I know that."

Suddenly the suite was flooded with light. Veronica brought her hand up and covered her eyes. Raj squinted as he made his way over to the wall and flipped the switch, plunging the room into candlelit darkness again. Then he turned on a couple of lamps while Veronica blew out the candles.

She put her hands on her hips, frowned. "Perhaps we should have kept the candles. More romantic."

Someone pounded on the door and Veronica jumped, squeaking as she did so.

Raj went and peeked through the hole, then jerked the door open when he saw it was Brady.

"Where is she?"

Raj stepped back. "She's here."

Brady burst into the room and rushed to Veronica's side. Raj watched them carefully as Brady swept her into a bear hug. "I'm so glad you're well," he said before he set her down again.

She smoothed a hand over her pajamas. Self-consciously? Probably, since Brady had found her alone here with him and she was clearly dressed for bed. Though how she could think elf pajamas were the least bit suggestive, Raj wasn't sure.

"I'm fine, Brady."

Brady shoved a hand through his hair. He was a tall man, though not as tall as Raj, and he'd remained lean throughout the years. Brady's hair was graying at the temples, but that was the only change Raj had noted since the last time—before tonight—that he'd seen the other man.

Brady threaded his fingers through Veronica's

and brought her hand to his lips. Raj didn't like
the tight pulse of envy that shot through him at
the casual gesture.

"I had a call I had to take," Brady said. "And
then the lights went out. I had hoped Raj had
you safe, but when I came to your room the first
time, you weren't here."

"We were, um, elsewhere," she said, not quite
meeting his gaze. "But I'm fine. Raj is a very
good bodyguard."

Brady's expression was fierce. "I'm glad you
think so. Clearly, the one you had tonight was
no good."

She looked angry suddenly. Deliberately, she
pulled her hand from Brady's grip, crossing her
arms over her chest. "So you knew about that?"

"I don't question Raj's methods," Brady said.
"He's never failed me."

Veronica slapped him on the shoulder. It
wasn't hard. It was the kind of slap Raj imagined a sister would give to her annoying brother.

"That's for not telling me what you were
planning," Veronica said, her brows two angry
slashes in her face, though her tone was gentler
than Raj had expected it would be.

Brady, however, looked like a puppy who'd
peed on the carpet. He knew he wasn't in big

trouble, but he was in trouble nevertheless. And he didn't like it.

Poor Brady. The way he looked at Veronica, spoke about Veronica—he seemed to want more than her friendship, but he'd decided to be satisfied with what she gave him. Even now he looked at her as if she was the sun and he one of the lucky planets in her orbit.

Typical with women like her, Raj thought sourly. She drew men like flowers drew honeybees.

His mother had been exactly like that before she'd lost her beauty from the drugs and drinking.

Until then, however, she'd managed to keep them both warm and dry by dragging him to stay with her various "boyfriends."

There'd never been a shortage of men willing to take her in. They'd taken him by extension. Some had ignored him. Others had resented him. And at least one had threatened him.

"I knew you wouldn't approve," Brady was saying to her.

"I wouldn't have," she admitted. "But Raj has managed to show me the error of my ways."

Brady's gaze slewed to him. "Has he?"

Veronica was looking over Brady's shoulder at him with wide eyes. She gave her head a little shake, as if to warn him. Raj knew what she wanted from him. And he had no problem complying, because the fewer people who knew about the doll, the better.

Raj shrugged. "She was stubborn at first, but I pointed out that if I'd come to kill her, I'd have been able to do so with very little trouble once I'd got rid of her bodyguard."

Brady heaved a sigh as he turned back to her. "I knew you'd be sensible, Veronica."

"She is very sensible," Raj said as Veronica's cheeks turned pink. No doubt she was remembering how *in*sensible she'd been until she'd discovered the doll. She turned and went to sit on the couch, once more the cool, imperious lady.

An imperious lady in elf pajamas. He had to bite down on the inside of his cheek to keep from laughing at the incongruity.

"So what now?" Brady asked.

"I'm staying close," Raj said. "Veronica doesn't want her staff to know she has extra security, so we've decided to pretend there's a bit of a...uh, relationship."

Brady blinked. His gaze raked over Raj, as if just now realizing he was without his tie and jacket, and then he turned to Veronica. She heaved a sigh. "Don't look at me that way, Brady. It's the only way to keep this a secret.

Raj will pretend to be my newest boyfriend. It makes the most sense."

"Is that wise? You're the President of Aliz now," Brady said.

Veronica tilted her head back and threaded her fingers through that glorious platinum hair. "Yes, well, I'm allowed a bit of a personal life. And besides, it's not really true. Raj is undercover."

Brady seemed to take the news in stride when it came from her. Naturally. "I suppose you're right." Then he turned to Raj, his eyes sparking. "Raj, a word, if you don't mind?"

Veronica rolled her eyes. "For God's sake, you're the one who orchestrated this in the first place. It's all strictly professional—isn't that right, Raj?"

Raj's blood hummed. Electricity crackled in his veins, but whether it was irritation with his old friend or something to do with Veronica, he wasn't quite sure.

"You know I don't get involved with clients, Brady. Have I ever let you down?"

The other man shook his head. "Not so far."

Raj heard the undertones that seemed to say, *But this woman is different. Irresistible. You'll get involved, and you'll slip up somehow at the job.*

"Do you want my involvement or not?" Raj said mildly.

"I do, but I thought you had people for this."

Ironic, since Raj had originally suggested one of VSI's teams and Brady had said he wanted Raj personally. "A team won't be able to uphold the necessary fiction. The client wants it kept quiet. This is the best way."

Brady gave him a look that held volumes of meaning. "Whatever it takes to keep her safe."

"That's the idea."

Brady stayed awhile longer, chatting with Veronica, while Raj kept in contact with his people. Her staff was scattered throughout the hotel, but they were beginning to make their way back.

There were only eight people with her. A small number, but Aliz was a small country. Besides, it would make it easier to have them watched.

Within half an hour, they'd all trickled back to Veronica's suite. He sat by and watched Veronica interact with them, surprised that she seemed so cool and controlled as she did so. He'd had the doll removed and the room checked thoroughly, so nothing was out of place.

He watched for signs of guilt or surprise in anyone, but there seemed to be nothing. The guard who'd abandoned his post arrived, but his guilt was most certainly of a different nature.

Veronica's chief of staff, a man named Georges, dealt with the man quickly and effectively. He was ordered to pack his bags and told he would be returning to Aliz on the next available flight.

And then everyone was gone again. Brady said his goodbyes as Raj sipped the coffee that Martine, Veronica's secretary, had prepared for him. Veronica walked with Brady to the door. He gave her a kiss on both cheeks, and then—after shooting Raj another meaningful look—he was gone, too.

"Ready for bed, darling?" Raj said, setting down the coffee.

She looked at him haughtily. He almost laughed. But he was glad to see her be strong, glad that she wasn't succumbing to the terror and uncertainty. She'd played her part quite well tonight. Once her people had returned, she'd acted as if nothing had happened. He—and whoever had put the doll there for her to find—were the only ones who knew.

"Don't get carried away with your part," she told him.

And then she sagged against the door, raised

a shaking hand to her head. Raj was moving before he ever realized he'd stood.

Veronica's heart crashed against her rib cage as she watched him. He moved like a cat, so sleek and deadly, coming straight for her. She was frozen in place, watching the way the fabric of his shirt stretched across his chest, molding the hard curves beneath. Her mouth went dry at the thought of what lay beneath the crisp white material.

She rubbed her palm over her eyes. What was she doing thinking of him naked when some maniac had gotten inside her room and put a defiled doll on her bed?

"Don't go there," he said firmly, reaching her side and putting an arm around her shoulders. "Don't give it power over you."

"I'm trying," she whispered. Because it was so cruel, so evil. Reminding her of what she'd lost.

Of what she'd destroyed.

Because she was the one responsible for what had happened to her baby, wasn't she? If she'd known she was pregnant sooner, she wouldn't have continued to drink cocktails or stay out until the early-morning hours, partying with her so-called friends because she couldn't bear to be alone.

It didn't matter what the doctor told her. She knew it was her fault.

"You need to sleep," Raj said, his arm firm around her. She wanted to turn into his embrace, wanted to bury her face against his solid chest again. She'd felt so safe for those few minutes earlier when she'd done so. "When was the last time you had a good night's rest?"

Veronica shrugged as he herded her toward the bedroom. "I don't remember. I sleep, but not well."

She hadn't slept well in months. Not since she'd realized what a truly horrible person she was.

"Then get into your bed and try."

She stopped at the threshold to the bedroom. "I can't sleep in there tonight."

He skimmed a hand along her jaw, the touch warm and light. It made her insides tighten. Heat—glorious heat—leeched into her bones. How could she need his touch when she didn't even know him?

"I'm not going anywhere. You'll be safe."

"I don't really want to sleep with you, Raj," she said, though she realized it was a bit of a lie. Right now, she was tempted to seek oblivion in his arms, tempted to drive away her memories by using his body for one hot night of sex.

"We aren't sleeping together," he replied. "But I'll be here nonetheless."

"Where are you planning to sleep, then?" she asked.

"The couch folds out."

She swallowed. He would be here, sharing the same space but not quite sharing it. She had to admit that she felt safe at the thought—as well as a bit unnerved.

"It's happening so fast," she said, shaking her head. "By tomorrow, every newspaper and tabloid will be simultaneously writing about our grand affair and our inevitable breakup."

"Not quite yet. We have a day or two with this snowstorm keeping everyone busy."

She snorted. "I wish I had your confidence. Not that it matters," she said. "I don't really care what they say, so long as you find whoever did this."

"I will," he said in that sexy voice of his that sent little whirlpools of heat spiraling down her spine.

Veronica dropped her gaze again, unable to keep looking at him. Up close, those golden eyes made her long for things she had no right to long for. Made her reckless, dizzy and willing to do things she hadn't ever thought she'd do again.

"I don't want to sleep in that bed tonight. Do you suppose we could trade?"

His sigh was long-suffering. "We can't trade because this is the exterior room. But you can have the fold-out bed. I'll take the floor."

She lifted her head again, her eyes meeting his. He was so solemn, so serious. "I can't ask you to do that."

He shrugged. "It's fine. I'll drag the covers from the other bed. Believe me, I've slept in worse places than on a floor."

She helped him remove cushions and unfold the bed from the couch. Once that was made, he disappeared into her bedroom and came back with a pile of blankets and pillows that he laid out on the floor nearby.

She felt guilty as she climbed into the cozy bed, and yet she couldn't bear to sleep in the other room. She'd thought she could, but she couldn't.

And tomorrow, she was going to play the diva and demand another room. At least her reputation was good for something.

"Raj," she said once the light was out and everything was quiet again.

"Yes?"

"Where did you sleep that was worse than a floor?"

"You don't really want to know."

"I wouldn't have asked otherwise. Though if you don't want to say, that's a different matter."

She heard him sigh. "I was in the military, Veronica. The Special Forces. I've slept in mud, blood, blazing deserts and freezing blizzards. A floor in a posh hotel is heavenly."

"I still feel badly for taking your bed," she said.

"Then invite me into it."

She couldn't help but smile. "You say that to shut me up. I heard what you said to Brady."

"Maybe I lied."

Her heartbeat throbbed in the darkness. "I don't believe you."

"Invite me into your bed and find out."

Flames licked her skin at the thought. "Good night, Raj," she said, punching her pillow and turning onto her side.

She wasn't sure, but she thought he laughed softly. "Sleep well, Veronica."

There wasn't much chance of that now that he'd planted the image in her head of the two of them in this bed together. Skin against skin, heat against heat, soft against hard.

She practically moaned at the thought.

CHAPTER FIVE

LONDON was beautiful in the snow, especially Hyde Park with all its trees and open expanses. Though it was dark, the snow made everything bright and fresh. Veronica knew that it wouldn't necessarily look so pristine during the day when all the warts and blemishes of humanity shone through.

But for now, she could enjoy it as her limousine crawled its way toward Mayfair and the exclusive party she'd been invited to there.

Tonight, she hoped to persuade Giancarlo Zarella, the Italian hotel baron, to bring one of his exclusive resorts to Aliz. Where Giancarlo went, others would follow.

But rather than concentrating on the Italian and going over the information about him that she'd been given, she kept thinking of Raj. She had not seen him since this morning.

He'd shaken her awake early, telling her they had to put the bed away before her secretary arrived with the morning dispatches. She'd been bleary-eyed, but she'd obeyed.

Or, rather, she'd mostly watched while Raj fixed everything. Then he led her into the bedroom and told her to climb into the bed. In the gray light of morning, the bed hadn't looked so frightening. She'd complied, falling asleep immediately.

When she'd awakened a second time—with a hotel maid delivering her breakfast tray and Martine standing stoically near—Raj was gone. Brady arrived a bit later, and once she'd answered her dispatches and sent Martine on an errand, she'd quizzed Brady.

Raj Vala was not simply a bodyguard. He was self-made, the owner of Vala Security International, a very successful firm that provided elite corporate and internet security.

According to Brady, Raj was a loner. And he was every bit as hard and ruthless as she'd thought he would be, with a military Special Forces background and the drive to be the best in everything he did.

Raj, Brady assured her, would make sure she was completely protected from harm.

After last night, she tended to believe it. She took her phone from her purse and checked her text messages. She would not ever be caught without a personal phone again.

The text from Raj was still there, still brief and to the point: he would meet her at the party. She smoothed a hand down the sleek ice-blue Vera Wang dress she wore. It was strapless, slit up one side, and shimmered as if it had been sewn with millions of tiny lights.

She told herself she'd chosen it to appeal to Signor Zarella, but the truth was she'd been thinking of Raj. Her hair was tousled and long, flowing artfully around her face and over her shoulders. She checked her makeup in the small mirror she'd tucked into her purse and breathed deeply to control the racing of her heart.

It wasn't like her to be nervous. She'd always loved parties, always loved getting dressed up and going out with other people who laughed and talked and helped her feel as if she were catching up on everything she'd missed growing up.

Except that now, part of her wished she could be anywhere but here. The thought of mingling with yet another crowd failed to cheer her the way it once would have.

The limo arrived at the Witherstons' grand Georgian town house, and Veronica deliberately turned her thoughts to Giancarlo Zarella. She had a duty to perform. Obsessing over her personal issues wouldn't help her to get it done.

Her bodyguard—a different man from yesterday—preceded her from the car. Three other Alizeans exited a car that had been following and formed a loose band around her. They were all very serious about their jobs today.

After they went inside and Veronica gave her thanks to the host and hostess, her security team peeled away until she was left with one man following at a discreet distance.

Inside the ornate ballroom, she was swept into the whirl and chatter of the crowd. Men and women introduced themselves in dizzying succession, her hostess having appeared from somewhere to guide her through the maze. She was still hoping to talk with Signor Zarella when Mrs. Witherston gave a little gasp.

"Madam President," she said breathlessly, "allow me to introduce you to Raj Vala."

Veronica turned sharply, her gaze clashing with Raj's. He was smiling at her as if he'd never seen her before in his life.

"Pleased to meet you, Madam President," Raj said.

"Likewise, Mr. Vala," Veronica replied, following his lead.

But her heart began to beat double time as

she took him in. He was far too handsome in his bespoke tuxedo, the white shirt once more setting off the golden color of his skin and eyes.

Truly, it should be against the law for a man to be so striking.

The jazz ensemble struck up a tune and Raj reached for her before she realized what he was about. "Do me the honor, Madam President?" he asked, as Mrs. Witherston tittered like a Regency matron.

"Of course," she said as she put her hand in his. What else could she say? What else did she *want* to say?

Raj swept her into the swirling crowd, one hand firmly against her back, the other clasping hers. The pressure of his touch comforted her, made her feel as if she'd come home again after a long time away.

She hated it. Hated how her body reacted, how her mind seemed to want to attach significance to this man. He might be able to keep her physically safe from harm, but he could not keep her safe from himself if she insisted on lying helplessly in the tiger's claws.

She knew better, and yet she turned into a puddle each time he touched her.

"How have you been today?" he asked.

"Well," she said. "You?"

His eyes seemed to search her face, as if he didn't quite believe her. "I was busy taking care of a few things. But now I'm all yours," he said, a devilish grin lifting the corners of his sensual mouth.

"Oh, all mine," she cooed. "How delightful, Mr. Vala."

"I thought we had gone beyond that."

"How could we? I've only just met you."

Her heart skipped a beat at his sudden smile. "Ah, yes, of course. I thought we could use this opportunity to begin our 'official' relationship."

"Why not?" she said, returning his smile. "It's certainly more dignified."

"But perhaps it's not the first time we've met," he said, his gaze skimming her face as he brought her hand up to his mouth and kissed it. "Perhaps we are old souls who have known one another before. Perhaps we are meant to be."

Veronica stumbled, but quickly caught herself. Raj was frowning. "It's the shoes," she said. And the fact she was tired from a restless night and unnerved to be in his arms again. "I'm fine."

"Good," he said. They moved across the floor together, their steps as fluid as silk. In her peripheral vision, she could see people stopping, pointing, heads leaning together as they talked about her and Raj. Ah, well, that had been the plan, had it not?

And yet it disappointed her in some respects. Now that they would be publicly linked, it was as if the innocence of their budding relationship had been eroded.

What relationship?

"Are we falling madly in love now?" Raj asked, jolting her out of her thoughts.

"Madly," she agreed, playing the game. "I've never felt like this before."

"Neither have I."

The words they said had no meaning, and yet she couldn't help but want to assign meaning that wasn't there. Had she ever been truly, madly in love before? She'd thought she'd been in love, but she'd usually realized the disappointing truth at some stage.

And she was positive that no man had ever felt that emotion for her. Lust, yes. Love, no.

"When we finish dancing, I suppose you will remain by my side the entire night?" she asked. "Enraptured by my presence?"

"The proverbial wild horses could not drag me away, Madam President." He lifted her hand to his lips again. The feather touch of his mouth against her skin sent a shudder rolling through her body. Hot need sizzled into the deepest parts of her.

Too bad this really wasn't Regency England, because then she would be wearing long gloves. She wouldn't be able to feel the sensual pressure of his mouth on her skin, wouldn't have to fight the focusing of all her senses upon that one spot. It was an exquisite torture to endure.

"Too bad our love is doomed to fail," she said, needing to counteract the drugging affect of his touch.

Again with the killer smile. "Then let us enjoy it while it lasts," he purred. "It's much more fun that way."

The evening went much as she'd thought it might. Raj did not leave her side. To all appearances, he was smitten with her. And she returned the favor, smiling in his direction, seeking him out if he walked away for the barest moment. Her eyes were pulled to him as if he were a magnet and she the metal.

It made talking to Giancarlo Zarella a bit difficult, but she finally managed to get the Italian alone at a table for a few moments. He seemed interested in Aliz, his eyes gleaming speculatively as she talked of incentives and subsidies.

"You would levy no taxes against us for the first year of operations, you say?"

Giancarlo was handsome, but she found herself comparing him to Raj and judging him lacking. "So long as you invest the money into building up the resort and hiring Alizeans to staff it."

"Make it two years, and I will consider it," he said shortly.

Veronica leaned in. "One year is what I can promise. But I pledge to work on reducing the tax burden in your next five years in Aliz."

Giancarlo laughed. "You drive a hard bargain," he said. "But then you know just how to twist the knife enough to get me to notice. I will think on it, I promise you."

After that, Veronica felt as if nothing could puncture the balloons lifting her up tonight. She had no guarantees, but she felt as if she'd made a good start with Giancarlo. He would be in touch, she was certain. He left her at the table with an apology as someone beckoned him from another table a bit farther away.

"Did you get what you wanted?"

Veronica jumped at the voice. Raj was frowning down at her. He seemed troubled, but not alarmingly so. "I did," she replied. "Or so I think."

He took her elbow and helped her up. "Good. I think it is time we leave, then."

Veronica blinked. The jazz ensemble was playing an upbeat version of a classic Christmas carol. "Time we leave? I'm not finished here yet."

"How many hearts do you plan to capture tonight?" he asked. His voice was teasing, but his eyes seemed hot and intense. Serious. "You've had a long few days. It's time you rest."

"I can decide that for myself. You weren't hired to oversee my schedule, you know." She knew he was merely trying to protect her from harm, and yet the memories of her life with her father were too strong to dismiss. She would not be so controlled ever again. Keeping her safe wasn't the same as wrapping her in a cocoon.

His jaw hardened imperceptibly. "Actually, it goes with the territory. Or didn't you realize that?"

"I decide when I leave," she said. "And I'm not ready yet. Unless there is a real threat at this moment and time, which I will acknowledge is your responsibility. Is there?"

He looked angry. "No," he said shortly. "There is no immediate threat."

"Then we stay."

One eyebrow crooked. The superiority of that look infuriated her. "Then don't blame me when you encounter people you might wish you had not."

"And what's that supposed to mean?"

"It means that Andre Girard just arrived."

Her heart skipped a beat at that name falling from Raj's lips. It was wrong somehow. Horribly, horribly wrong. For a moment she wondered if he knew what had happened between her and Andre, but then she told herself it wasn't possible. Only a very small handful of people knew the true story.

"Andre is old news," she said, more to convince herself than him. "I will not leave a party simply because he's here, too."

At that moment, Raj changed tactics. He slipped an arm around her waist, anchoring her to his side as he smiled down at her, his head dipping so close to her own that if she tilted her head back just slightly, their lips would meet. Her heart thundered in her breast so hard she was certain he could see it.

"I'm glad he's old news," he said softly. "Because he's on his way over here."

Veronica couldn't speak as a shiver skidded along her nerve endings.

"I don't care," she finally managed to say.

"Good," Raj said. "Neither do I."

Then he dipped his head and kissed her.

Veronica couldn't have prepared herself for the sensations zinging through her even if she'd had a year to do so. Raj's mouth on hers was firm, the pressure exquisite. The barest slip of his tongue along the seam of her lips, and she was opening to him, taking him inside, tangling her tongue with his.

He made a sound of approval low in his throat that vibrated through her. Her core was melting, softening, aching. It was both surprising and alarming.

She knew there were reasons she shouldn't be seen kissing this man so publicly, but she couldn't think of even one. He scrambled her senses with his nearness. Made her long for more of the same. Made her want bare skin on bare skin, bodies tangled and straining together toward a single goal.

His fingers splayed over her jaw, tilted her head back so he could better access her mouth. The kiss seemed to go on and on, and yet she knew it had to have been only a matter of seconds before it ended.

She was staring up at him now, her lips stinging, her pulse throbbing in places she'd thought dead and buried until he'd walked into her life just twenty-four hours ago.

Raj was so cool, so unaffected. His golden

eyes were hot, but that was the only sign he'd been at all moved by their kiss. He took a step back, his arm looped loosely around her.

"So you've found a new victim, I see."

Veronica turned. Andre smirked at her, a pouty supermodel clinging to his arm. Andre was slick and handsome, as always. But he didn't move her, not anymore. What she'd once thought was a fun and witty personality was now tarnished and dull.

Or, rather, her eyes had been opened to his true nature.

"Andre. I would say it's a pleasure to see you again, but we'd both know that was a lie."

Andre laughed. "It was good while it lasted, no? And just look at you now," he said. "President of Aliz. However did you pull that one off, darling?"

Veronica refused to rise to the bait. It was what he wanted, but she relished denying him his wish. "The usual way. I ran against the incumbent and the people decided I was the better choice."

"Ah, yes." His eyes narrowed. "So much more interesting than motherhood, I would imagine."

Veronica kept smiling even as a hot dagger of pain twisted in her gut. She wanted to turn into Raj's chest, hide until Andre was gone, but she would not. She would not give her former lover the satisfaction of reacting.

She'd known he would take the shot. From the moment Raj had told her Andre was here, she'd known what would happen. She could feel Raj's curiosity sparking, but she had to ignore it. Andre was her problem, not his.

"I believe there are rewards in many things," she said.

Andre's gaze flicked to Raj. "Careful, my friend. She's not at all what she seems. You think she wants what you want, until one day she surprises you by wanting something else. If you're lucky, you will escape before then."

Raj's grip on her waist tightened. "Veronica is an amazing woman," he said. "Too bad that you couldn't see it. Good for me, though. So thanks for being an idiot."

Warmth flooded her. She knew he was only playing a part, but she was still grateful to him for saying it. He could have said nothing, but he'd chosen to defend her. When was the last time anyone had done so?

She'd been so devastated after she'd lost the baby. And yes, she'd turned to Andre, thinking he might feel her pain, too. But he hadn't cared one bit. He'd considered it a lucky escape.

Andre's smile was patently false. "Suit your-self," he said. "But don't say I didn't warn you."

Then he turned and walked away, the model trotting along dutifully.

Veronica let out the breath she hadn't real-ized she'd been holding. It had gone better than she'd expected, though perhaps she should have realized that Andre would never make a scene. It simply wasn't his style to get overly worked up about anything.

"What did you ever see in that guy?"

She met Raj's critical gaze. He looked at her as if she'd grown a second head and he was try-ing to reconcile it. Veronica shrugged self-con-sciously. "He was charming when we first met. We had fun together."

Belatedly, she pulled out of Raj's grip, the memory of their kiss still sizzling into her brain. He let her go easily enough, and it made her wonder if she was the only one who'd been af-fected by the contact. That kiss had stripped away all her barriers while it lasted. It had scorched her to the depths of her soul.

Raj, however, looked completely cool and controlled. As if it had meant nothing to him.

Veronica lifted her chin. She was tired and she'd had enough for tonight. Enough with pre-tense and drama. Enough with being *Madam*

President. She'd done what she came to do. "I'm ready to leave now."

To his credit, Raj only said, "I had thought you might be."

It took a while to say her goodbyes, but eventually they were in the foyer and Raj was helping her into her coat while her bodyguard stood by. She'd assumed he would put her into the car and follow separately, but he climbed into the warm interior with her. The guard went into the front seat, and then they were rolling away from Mayfair, the darkened London streets still alive with sound and traffic even at this late hour.

The kilometers ticked by in silence, other than the street sounds coming from outside. Veronica turned her head and watched as snow drifted silently down. She thought about making small talk, but could suddenly think of nothing to say.

"You will have to tell me eventually," Raj said, his voice like the crack of a gun in the silent car, though he spoke in a normal tone. It was the sound coming after so much silence that startled her and made her lift a shaking hand to her throat to fuss with her scarf.

"Tell you what?" she managed to respond. Her voice was even. Calm. She was proud of that.

Raj's fingers suddenly threaded into hers, closed tightly. They both wore gloves, but the pressure of his grip was warm, soothing. Comforting.

He squeezed softly, as if he were imparting strength. "About the baby."

CHAPTER SIX

She didn't say anything for so long that he wondered if she'd heard him. But of course she had. She sat stiffly, her head still turned away from him. In the light of one of the buildings they passed, he saw her throat move.

Raj pulled off his glove and put his fingers against her cheek. She turned to him, her eyes filled with tears. His fingers were wet and his heart constricted at the pain on her face.

"I don't want to talk about this with you," she said, her voice barely more than a whisper.

"I'm sorry," he said softly. He didn't want to push her, and yet he had to know. "But it could be important."

She closed her eyes, shook her head slightly. Her platinum hair gleamed in the dim light, and he thought of her last night, standing by her bed and calling for him. How vulnerable she'd looked, how innocent. Such a contrast with the woman he'd gotten acquainted with on paper.

Her chin dropped, as if she were surrendering. He found a box of tissues in a nearby compartment and handed them to her. She snatched a few into her hand and dabbed at her face.

"How can it be important?" she finally said. "No one really knows about it."

"Someone does. Andre does."

She sucked in a breath on a half sob. "Of course he knows. He was the father."

Somehow, though he'd expected it, that news sliced through his gut like a sword. He didn't want to think of Veronica with Andre Girard, didn't want to imagine that she could have loved the man once. But she must have done so.

"Was he angry?" He still didn't quite know what they were talking about, but he could tease the details from her if he worked gently enough.

Her laugh was bitter. "Angry? God, no. More like relieved. He didn't want a child, so he's not in the least bit upset there isn't one."

"I'm sorry for your loss, Veronica." He squeezed her hand again. He wanted to pull her into his arms and hold her tight, but he wasn't sure she wanted him to do so. Instead, he sat and waited.

"You're good," she said, dabbing at her eyes again. "You've managed to get me to talk about it after all. No matter that I don't want to."

"I have no wish to cause you pain," he said. "But I need to understand who could want to hurt you. Whoever it is knows about the baby. And this person sees it as the perfect way to get to you."

Her free hand clenched into a fist on her lap. "I wish I could understand why. It has nothing to do with anyone but me and Andre."

"Was there another woman? A jealous ex, perhaps?"

"There's always a jealous ex. But why would anyone care enough to be so cruel when we're no longer together? We weren't even very serious, but then I got pregnant and—"

"And what?" he prompted when she didn't continue.

She bent forward as if she were in pain, rocked back and forth, her face turned away from him. It alarmed him. His throat felt tight as he waited.

A sob escaped her, but she stuffed her fist against her mouth and breathed hard, as if trying to cram the rest of them down deep.

Raj put an arm around her, pulled her toward him. She turned instantly, buried her face against him.

"I'm sorry," she said, her voice muffled and broken.

"It's all right," he said softly. "It's all right."

A lump formed in his throat as he watched the lights of storefronts go by. He had no idea where they were, or how long they were silent, before she pushed away from him and dabbed her eyes.

As if she hadn't just cried her heart out. As if she hadn't turned to him for comfort while she did so.

She was an enigma to him. Soft and hard at once. Strong and weak. Filled with sadness and pain. Not at all what he'd expected from the party girl in the tabloids.

If anything, he realized how very fragile she was beneath the layers of steel she cloaked herself in. He had no right to try and break through those barriers.

"I lost the baby soon after I learned I was pregnant," she said. She shook her head, swallowed hard. He could hear the audible gulp as she pushed her sobs down deep again. But then she speared him with a look. "I won't break, Raj. I'm stronger than you think. And I won't let anyone use this to stop me from doing what's best for Aliz."

Her mind worked much more quickly than he'd given her credit for only yesterday, when he'd watched her work the crowd from his position in the bar. He'd thought her pampered and shallow, but he had to admit that she had depths he'd never guessed at.

"Who is the woman in the tabloid reports?" he asked. "Because I can hardly credit she's the same person as the woman sitting beside me now."

"Oh, no, she's definitely the same. Some of it is exaggerated, of course. But much of it is true." He wondered if she knew she was rubbing her thumb along the underside of his palm. The pressure was light, but it made him want to strip her glove off and see what her touch would feel like on his skin.

"I can hardly believe it," he said, trying to lighten the conversation once more.

"That was my version of acting out," she said quietly. "My rebellion against my father. The worse I behaved, the angrier he got. Did you ever act out, Raj?"

Her question surprised him. A dart of pain caught him behind the breastbone. "I think everyone has," he said.

Except that he hadn't. Not really.

He'd always had to be the adult in the house, especially once his mother started experimenting with drugs the summer he turned twelve. If he hadn't made sure they had food and a roof over their heads, however temporary, they'd have starved or frozen to death.

He'd known nothing but responsibility from the time he was young. He'd been stripped of a normal childhood by his mother's addictions and constant need for attention.

Acting out had been the furthest thing from his mind when all he'd cared about was food and shelter. Not that he could admit that to Veronica. It made him seem pitiful—and he definitely wasn't pitiful.

"Yes, I suppose so," she said. "Some of us worse than others, perhaps. But those days are over now, at least for me. I have too many things I want to do in life. I've wasted enough time."

Raj stifled a laugh. "You're twenty-eight and the president of your nation. How have you wasted time?"

Her smile was unexpected. It shook at the corners, as if she were still on the verge of tears.

It made him want to kiss her again. A white-hot bolt of need shot through him as he watched her mouth.

"That's true, yes. But I'm realizing what I really want. I'm only sorry it took me so long to figure it out."

"And what is it you want, Veronica?" Because he knew what he wanted right this minute. He wouldn't act on it, of course. Kissing her at the party had been one thing. Kissing her now that they were alone was another altogether.

"You will laugh."

"I won't."

"You will, but it's okay. I want a home. A real home, with a family. Maybe it'll just be a cat or a dog, or maybe I'll find a man I adore, who adores me in return. But I want the dream, the happy-ever-after where I like who I am and someone agrees with me."

Raj swallowed. Home. Family. He had no idea what those things were, really, other than a roof and four walls, and people whose happiness and welfare you were responsible for. "It's a nice dream. I hope you get it."

"You think it's ridiculous," she said.

"No."

"You do."

He sighed. "It's not that. It's just that I doubt you've ever been without a home. You want to imbue the word with more than it needs. You want it to fulfill you emotionally when, really, that is your responsibility."

Her thumb had stilled in his palm. Gently, she disentangled her hand from his and he knew he'd gone too far. Or maybe he'd gone far enough. It was better if she had no illusions about him.

Better if they nipped this growing attraction in the bud and kept their relationship on the professional level it was meant to remain on.

"You're a cynic," she said. "I hadn't realized it."

"Not a cynic. A realist. Home isn't a magical place. It's shelter. It's having enough to eat, being warm. You have always had these things in abundance. Not everyone is so lucky."

She bowed her head. "No, you're right. I've never gone without the necessities. But I was talking of something more. Something intangible."

The car drew to a halt then and the door opened. They'd arrived back at the hotel she'd moved to earlier in the day. He thought he should say something more, should soothe her somehow—but he was at a loss. Instead, he exited and held his hand out for her.

"I thought you would understand," she said as she joined him on the curb, gazing up at him, her lovely face puzzled.

"I do," he said, because he had to say something. "I just don't happen to agree. Be thankful you've never slept on the street, or wondered where your next meal was coming from. Be thankful you've never had to fight for a dirty blanket to keep warm with because it was that or nothing. You are free to be you, wherever you happen to be. You already have what you need."

She sucked in a breath. The air misted around her face as she let it out again. She looked sad. "I hadn't quite thought of it like that."

"Many people don't."

"Maybe because it's easier to think that if only we have X, then Y will happen."

He was surprised at how readily she accepted the idea. And it made him feel somewhat guilty, as well. She'd been through a lot recently. More than she'd told him, and it wasn't his right to make her question the ideas that comforted her.

"I'm sorry, Veronica."

Her brows drew together. "For what? For speaking the truth? For reminding me of all the advantages I've had?"

He put his hands on either side of her face, gloried in the soft catch of her breath. She wanted him as much as he wanted her. It was enough. It would have to be enough, because he could not act upon it. Even if she weren't under his protection, he couldn't take her to his bed.

Because she'd been through too much pain and loss, and because she wanted more than he could give. He could see it in her eyes. Hell, she'd just said it aloud. Veronica was a woman who wanted a family.

The one thing he felt unqualified to ever provide. Family wasn't for him.

"I'm sorry for making you question what you want," he said. "There's nothing wrong with building a safe place in your head, and with trying to get there. Sometimes, X does lead to Y."

"You're really sweet," she replied softly.

He wanted to laugh. Sweet? Him? No way. "If it makes you happy to think so, then, yes, I'm sweet."

She giggled, then slapped her hand over her mouth as if she were surprised she'd done so. It was as if she'd let him see the real Veronica for a moment, the one beneath the pain and mystery. He'd had glimpses of her before, but never so natural as this. A sharp pain settled beneath his rib cage and refused to go away.

"As sweet as a tiger," she said a moment later. "A tiger who's just eaten and won't be hungry for a while."

He couldn't help but return her smile, though his chest ached. She was infectious like that. "Oh, I'm definitely hungry," he said. "But I have excellent self-control."

"I'm glad to hear it." She ducked her head so their eyes no longer met. And then she delivered what would have been the death blow had he been a weaker man. "Because I seem to have none at all when it comes to you."

A moment later she was striding into the hotel, leaving him standing numbly on the sidewalk. Aching. Wanting. Cursing himself.

Veronica woke up in the night, gasping for breath, the tail of some dream fading away. The air was dry, so dry, and her throat hurt. She didn't care how cold it was, she needed to open a window, needed that fresh bite of outside air to cleanse her. She stumbled to the window and found the mechanism—then she was cranking the window up and the air rushing in made her gasp again.

But it felt good. Clean.

She stood at the sill, shivering, but feeling refreshed nonetheless. She couldn't even remember the dream now.

The door to her bedroom burst open, a bright light searing into her brain. It happened so fast she wasn't able to let out even a squeak of surprise. The light winked out again and a voice asked, "What in the hell are you doing?"

Raj's voice. Relief slid through her, made her weak. If he'd been out to harm her, as he'd pointed out so recently, no one could have stopped him.

"What does it look like I'm doing?" she said.

Raj crossed the room so silently that when he arrived at her side, she jumped. Then he was cranking the window closed again.

"Hey," she said. "I want it open."

"Too bad," he replied. "It's not safe."

She could only blink into the blackness. But then light flooded the room as he snapped on her bedside lamp. The bright spots left from the light he'd shined when he'd first entered still marched across her vision. Big green splotches that made him indistinct if she looked directly at him. She turned her head, peered at him sideways.

He loomed, big and solid and oh, so unapproachable. He was completely different than he'd been earlier. He'd charmed her, held her, soothed her. Kissed her.

And now he was back to treating her as if she was something unappealing that he'd found on the bottom of his shoe.

Her temper sparked. "Do you mean to tell me that it's not safe if I open the window a crack on the tenth floor of a hotel? For a few minutes?"

"Precisely."

She popped her hands onto her hips. "What kind of world do you live in, Raj? Because I'm not sure I want to be a part of it."

"You already are," he said. For the first time,

she noticed that what she'd always assumed to be a mild British accent had taken on a distinctly American twist. "It's your world, not mine. You entered it when you ran for president. You bought it when you got elected."

What had gotten into him? Before she could dwell on it, something else occurred to her. "How did you know the window was open?"

"A small sensor," he said matter-of-factly.

A sensor. He'd put sensors in her room. She was familiar with that tactic. She'd been thinking of him when she'd dressed with such care tonight, and he'd been busy thinking of how to control her.

Her blood ran cold. She'd snuck out of her father's house once, when she was sixteen. He'd been so furious once he'd caught her that he'd had the place wired like a military compound.

Oh, yes, she knew about sensors.

Veronica worked hard to control her temper. What had happened to her as a teenager had nothing to do with now. She was someone who needed protecting, someone with big responsibilities. Raj had only been doing what she'd agreed to let him do.

"You could have told me," she said tightly. "I wouldn't have opened the window if I'd known."

His look was dark. "Most people don't open the window at 3:00 a.m. in the middle of winter."

"I won't be caged in," she said, panic rising in her throat as her insides clenched in fear. "I won't be controlled."

"Then you should have considered another career path," he said coldly.

She hugged her arms around her body. Her vision was still splotchy, but she could see that Raj was still in his tux. Or, partially in his tux. The jacket and tie were missing, and the top couple of studs were gone. His sleeves were rolled partway up his forearms. She realized that she'd never seen his bare arms before.

A shiver rippled over her.

Raj swore. "You'll catch a cold," he said gruffly as he came and put an arm around her, herded her toward the bed. "I thought you had more sense than this."

"I'm fine," she protested.

"Then why are you shaking?" he demanded.

She couldn't answer, not without giving away the secret of how he affected her. Because, though she was slightly chilled, it wasn't that making her shiver.

She wanted to shrug away from his touch, but couldn't. She was still so angry with him— and yet there was that electricity between them, that spark and fire that sizzled along her nerve endings the instant he touched her. It took her forcibly back to that moment outside the hotel when he'd told her he was hungry. Her insides had turned to jelly then. Her legs had wobbled. She'd wanted to take his hand and lead him to her bedroom.

She hadn't done it because she'd been confused. Did she want him because she felt close to him after the conversation in the car? Because she'd told him about the baby and she'd felt vulnerable? Because he'd held her hand and said he was sorry?

She wasn't sure, and in the end she'd done nothing.

But right now all the same thoughts and needs were crashing through her again. And she was asking herself once more how she could want this particular man when she'd wanted no man for over a year now.

Because he was wrong for her.

He was beautiful, strong, proud, fierce. And too wild to ever be tamed. No woman would ever own this man, and she was no longer willing to be the sort of woman who was temporary.

But oh, how her insides rippled and churned at his nearness. How her heart wanted the one thing that was forbidden to her.

He pulled the covers back and held them.

"Get in," he said. She obeyed because she was starting to shiver in earnest now. But she hardly believed it had anything to do with the ten seconds of fresh air, and everything to do with him.

"Don't think I did it because you told me to," she said when he dropped the covers on top of her.

His mouth twisted. "I would never think that, Veronica. You would just as soon die of exposure than do what I say. If you've gotten in bed, it's because you wanted to."

She closed her eyes. "Too right."

"Don't open the window again."

"I understood the first time," she said. "Raj?"

He turned back to her. "Yes?"

"Will you stay and talk to me for a little while?"

He didn't move, and she wondered if he would tell her no. But then he nodded, came over and sat on the edge of the bed farthest from her.

She didn't know why she'd asked him to stay, except that she'd suddenly not wanted to be alone. She couldn't remember her dream, but it hadn't been a good one. She felt restless, keyed up, anxious.

There was a time when she couldn't stand to be alone at all, when she'd had twenty-four-hour parties full of all the laughter, music and chatter she'd been denied growing up. She was no longer that person, but she still sometimes felt the weight of silence pressing in on her.

She deserved that silence, considering what she'd done. But tonight she couldn't handle it.

Veronica reached up and turned out the light, needing the anonymity of utter darkness. She could feel the solid presence of Raj nearby. Just like yesterday, it was comforting. She put a hand to her head, rubbed one temple. It was all the travel, all the days spent in hotels—all the days spent being serious and worrying about Aliz— that made her grateful for his company now.

She waited for him to speak, to say anything at all, but he didn't. She huffed out a sigh. "You aren't talking."

"Neither are you." She felt him move, the bed dipping as he slid up against the headboard and stretched out his legs.

"Where did you grow up?"

He muttered something beneath his breath. "Tell me about you. It's far more interesting."

"I disagree," she said. "I want to know why you sound British but sometimes use American phrases."

He blew out a breath. "My mother was American."

"See, that's interesting. Did you grow up in India?"

"No."

"Is it a secret?" she prompted when he said nothing else.

"No. But it's not important."

Veronica sighed. "Fine. Don't talk about it, then."

"I won't."

"I grew up in Aliz," she said, because she needed to say something. "I never left until I was eighteen. And then I didn't go back until my father's funeral two years ago."

"I'm sorry for your loss."

"Thank you. We weren't close, but we were… working on it…."

She'd tried to make her peace with her father. They'd been speaking more frequently in the months before his death. She sometimes couldn't believe he was gone. Though she understood now what had motivated him to be so overprotective, she'd had a hard time forgiving him for it.

"It's good you were trying."

"I think so." She turned on her side, facing Raj. She could see the outline of his profile in the dim light coming from the bedside clock. "What you're really wondering is why the people elected me president since I hadn't actually lived in Aliz for many years."

He didn't hesitate before answering. "I wonder why you ran, not why they elected you."

She thought of her father, of Paul Durand. Of the hope and delight she'd seen in the eyes of those Alizeans who believed in her ability to change things for the better. "I thought I could do something good for the country."

"I think you probably can," he said. "I think you already have."

For some reason, that made her throat tight. "I'm trying," she said. "It's very important to me."

She thought he laughed softly. "Veronica, I don't think there's anything in this world you can't do once you set your mind to it."

"I'm sure there are a few things," she said, her eyes stinging as her voice caught. *Damn it.* This was not at all what she'd intended when she'd started talking.

But this was how it had been since she'd lost her child. The yawning cavern snuck up on her when she least expected it, threatened to consume her.

Beside her, Raj swore again. And then he was moving, closing the distance between them and gathering her to him. She didn't protest, though she knew she should. How many times did she have to lose her composure in front of him?

Instead, she buried her nose in his pristine shirt and breathed him in. She loved being close to him.

"I'm sorry," he said. "I shouldn't have said that."

"No," she replied, her fingers curling into his shirt. "You were paying me a compliment. I liked it."

She could hear his heart thudding in his chest. It beat faster than she'd have thought. For some reason, that made her happy. Raj Vala—strong, amazing, sexy Raj—wasn't unaffected by holding her close. Perhaps he was a little bit human after all.

"But it made you think of what you'd lost."

She swallowed, unable to tell him the rest of it. Unable to say that she blamed herself and always would. "You can't guard what you say in hopes I won't."

His grip on her tightened. "I wish I could say something. Do something. I'd take away the hurt if I could."

She knew he meant it, and it touched her more than she could say. A lone tear seeped from her closed eyes and trickled down her cheek.

"Just hold me," she said. "It's enough."

CHAPTER SEVEN

Raj knew he was losing the battle with himself. He closed his eyes and tried to pretend he was somewhere—anywhere—but here, in her bed, holding her close and listening to her soft breathing. He felt the bite of moisture on his skin, knew she was crying. He wanted to make it stop, wanted her to sleep again. He didn't know how to make it happen.

She didn't make any sound, but her body trembled in his arms.

"Veronica," he said, his voice strangled, "it'll be okay. Someday, it'll be okay." He wasn't stupid enough to think that the kind of loss she'd suffered was something she would get over quickly. How could she? How could anyone?

Andre Girard was a fool. And Raj had a sudden desire to hunt the man down and make him suffer the way Veronica suffered. She shouldn't have to go through this alone.

"I know," she said, her voice so soft and

sweet, hovering on the edge of control. "I get upset sometimes, but it's normal."

He didn't know what was normal and what wasn't—but he couldn't stand that she was in pain. He tipped her chin up with his fingers, lowered his mouth to hers. He meant it to be a soft kiss, a sweet kiss. A kiss of comfort.

He should have known it was impossible.

Later, he wouldn't be able to recall who'd taken the kiss deeper first. But it didn't take more than a moment for it to happen. She clung to him, her mouth warm and inviting, her soft sigh like fuel to the fire stoking low in his belly.

He was harder than he'd ever been in his life. And he knew he was about to lose the battle between his head and his groin. He tried to remind himself of all the reasons he shouldn't be doing this…and came up empty.

He tightened his fingers in her hair—that glorious, lustrous fall of platinum silk—and gently pulled her head back as he broke the kiss. He had one chance left. One chance to end this free fall into insanity.

"Tell me no, Veronica. Tell me to get out, and I will. For both our sakes, tell me," he urged her. Because he was powerless so long as she clung to him. So long as she seemed to need his touch, his kiss, he was absolutely powerless to stop it.

He shouldn't be. He should be able to get up and walk away. He'd suffered unbelievable agony while training for the Special Forces, and he'd never broken. He'd endured.

But he couldn't endure her. She'd broken him, at least temporarily.

One word from her, and he could regain his strength. He could disentangle himself, distance himself. One word was all it would take.

"I can't," she said. "I don't want to. I want you to stay."

He groaned, and the sound reverberated through her body. Veronica's heart thundered in her ears. Heat prickled along the pathways of her nerves, slid deep into her senses, melted her core. She'd terrified herself with the words she'd spoken, and yet she'd known they were the right words.

She was ready for this again, ready for the intense pleasure of being with a man. With Raj. There were so many reasons why she shouldn't, why she should have said no as he'd told her to do, but she couldn't.

She simply couldn't.

He'd touched something inside her that had lain dormant for as long as she could remember. It was both shocking and compelling. Why now? Why him?

Why?

"I can't promise you anything beyond tonight," he said roughly. "You have to know that, Veronica. That's why you have to make me leave."

She reached up and spread her palm along the shadow of his jaw. He needed to shave, but she loved the rough texture.

"Just give me one night, then," she replied, surprising even herself with the request.

But he was untamable, this tiger. He needed to be free. She understood that. She would take what he could give her and then she would free him.

Veronica swallowed hard. For a moment, doubt assailed her. What was she doing? What was she getting herself into? Could she handle one night of passion between them? Was she really prepared for this?

But then he kissed her again, and she knew she was ready. Her body was on fire for him. Sizzled and sparked for him. Her pajamas—silk tonight—felt like sandpaper next to her sensitive skin. She wanted them off, and she wanted to burn herself up in his embrace.

In the dark of night, when no one would ever know.

When tomorrow came, she would deal with the aftermath.

His hand slid against the silk of her top, his fingers spreading to cup her breast. She moaned as he found and teased her nipple beneath the fabric. In answer, she tugged his shirt from his waistband, shoved her hands beneath it until she was touching the hot, smooth skin of his torso.

His groan whipped the froth of her excitement even higher. She struggled against the blankets, wanting to be free of them so she could wrap her body around his. He obliged her by grabbing a handful and yanking them down.

And then she was throwing a leg over his hip, pulling him to her. He rolled until he was on top of her, until that hard part of him she wanted so much was pressed intimately against the silk of her pajamas. In spite of the fabric between them, sensation streaked from her scalp to her toes when he flexed his hips and thrust against her.

His mouth—his beautiful, magical mouth—made love to hers so thoroughly that she never wanted to stop kissing him. For some men, kissing was a bothersome prelude to the main course. For other men—for this man—kissing was an erotic act in itself.

She'd never been kissed like this before. *Never.*

But she wanted more than his kiss. Veronica pushed his shirt up as high as she could make it go. She wanted their clothes gone, wanted to feel bare skin on bare skin. Raj broke the kiss, reached over his shoulder and tugged the shirt over his head with one hand. She could hear the studs snapping, the fabric tearing.

It was sexy and wild and she loved it. Her heart hammered, her pulse tripping as if she'd mainlined a vat of caffeine.

But oh, was he worth it.

His mouth found hers again, but his chest was now bare and she could run her hands over him. The hard planes and smooth skin, the dips and hollows of solid muscle that rippled beneath her fingers. So sexy.

Quickly, he unbuttoned her shirt, the fabric falling open until her breasts were exposed to his sight. She could see his eyes gleaming in the dim light coming from outside the windows. Her nipples peaked as he watched her. She was shameless. Utterly shameless.

"Raj," she said, his name a plea on her lips.

"You're beautiful, Veronica," he said softly, kissing her once more.

And then he was sliding his tongue down the column of her neck, kissing the sweet spot where the nerves in her shoulder seemed to connect to the hot, throbbing center of her. She arched her back, gasped.

Raj said something against her skin, but she didn't hear what it was. The vibrations rolled through her, crested in her core. If he kept doing that, she thought she might explode.

Impossible, but exciting. So exciting.

When his mouth closed over her nipple, she thought that was the end. How could she stand this much pleasure?

This much pain?

Because she couldn't help but think of all that had happened in the months since the last time she'd been with anyone. She'd changed so much. Fallen to the depths of despair. Risen again as she'd determined to go on with life.

Raj seemed to sense her turmoil. He chose that moment to slip his fingers beneath the waist of her pajama bottoms, and her temperature spiked. He made a noise of approval when he found the lacy top of her panties. Fire streaked through her. And *want,* so much want.

She thought she would die if he didn't touch her.

But he did, finding her swiftly, his fingers clever and sure as they stroked her while a long moan vibrated in her throat.

"Veronica," he groaned against her breast. "So sensitive, so responsive."

She couldn't speak, couldn't tell him it was all

because of him, because she trusted him. Wildly, she thought that she hardly knew him—and yet she knew enough. He was a good man, a strong man. He was reliable, even if he was ephemeral.

He was exactly what she needed when she needed it.

She would not think about tomorrow.

It didn't take long for her to reach the pinnacle; her body tightened so painfully—then flew free as she gasped his name.

His fingers stilled.

And then he was removing her bottoms, tossing them aside and pushing her legs apart. She thought he would unzip his trousers, would plunge into her body and join them together finally—but he did no such thing. Instead, he slid down until his mouth—that clever, beautiful mouth—hovered above her most sensitive spot. She could hardly breathe in anticipation of what came next.

She was not disappointed. His tongue slid over her, again and again, nibbling, sucking, flicking, while she grasped handfuls of the bedding and thrust her hips upward.

This time when she came apart, stars exploded behind her eyes. Her breath was sucked from her body as her back arched off the bed.

She was absolutely helpless beneath the on-slaught of pleasure.

He didn't stop there. He took her to the top again, then pushed her over the edge until she was ready to beg him to stop, to let her breathe, to let her recollect her senses and reorder them again.

It was simply too much. It was primal and raw, and as much as she wanted to stop, she also wanted to go on. She wanted to reach the next peak, and the next. But she wanted to soar with him instead of alone.

He must have felt something of her desire, because he kissed his way up her body again—her torso, her breasts, her shoulder…oh, that shoulder!—and back to her lips, capturing them for a long, lingering kiss.

Then he surprised her when he rolled to the side and tucked her against him. Confused, she pushed herself up with one hand splayed against his glorious chest. He was so dark in the night, so powerful and protective. She shivered in anticipated delight.

"We aren't finished yet," she said.

His laugh was strangled. "Yes, but I've realized I have no protection. This is not what I came here for tonight."

She leaned down and kissed him. "I'm on the

pill," she said against his lips. "I had to take it after…well, after I needed my hormones to stabilize. They were all over the place for a while."

His fingers came up and stroked along her cheek. It was a sweet gesture, so simple and honest. She loved it.

"You slay me, Veronica," he said. "And you deserve far better than I can give you. I'm humbled that you trust me, but you've just convinced me that I can't take advantage of your vulnerability."

She pulled away and sat up. She was completely naked, but she didn't care. Let him look. If it made him uncomfortable, so much the better. Frustration was a hot stew in her belly. And disbelief. Could he really be serious?

"You're the most arrogant man I've ever met, Raj Vala. And I've met some arrogant ones, believe me. What makes you think for one instant that I don't know what I want? That I can't make my own decisions? That I'm somehow blinded by your fabulousness and not in control of my own mind?"

"I didn't mean—"

"You did," she said firmly. "Because you're so wonderful, of course, and no woman can resist you. Therefore, it's up to you to be noble and deny my poor, weak female mind what it thinks it wants."

"You aren't thinking," he growled, "or you wouldn't want this. In the morning, you would regret it."

"That's my problem, isn't it?" she snapped, anger and sexual frustration building to a peak inside her. "You're here to protect me from an outside threat, not from myself."

"I want you, make no mistake. And if I were a bastard like Andre Girard—or any of those other men you've taken to your bed—I'd seize what you're offering me and to hell with your peace of mind."

"Fine," she said, scrambling from the bed and whirling to face him. She was absolutely on fire with anger. And humiliation. She'd thrown herself at him, and he'd turned her down flat. After making sure she had an orgasm or two—alone. It was ridiculous, but she felt so worthless right now.

"Clearly, you know what's best for me. Now get out and let me sleep."

He was so still and quiet that she didn't think he would respond, but a few seconds later he exploded off the bed, grabbing his torn shirt and coming to loom over her. "You'll thank me tomorrow," he snarled.

She started to snap back at him, but something stopped her. Sometimes you had to pull the thorn from the tiger's paw, right?

She put a palm on his chest, slid it up to his jaw. He shuddered beneath her touch, a great golden cat on the edge of control. Boldly, she reached for him, cupped her other hand around the bulge in his trousers.

"Veronica…"

"I'm a grown woman, Raj. I know what I want." She took a step closer to him then, her bare breasts coming into contact with his naked chest. "I need this," she told him. "Yes, you're the first after my loss, but that's why it has to be you. I do trust you, and I'm afraid I'll never find the courage again if you don't—" She sucked in a breath, her voice on the edge of breaking. It took her a few moments to regain control. "If you don't make love to me. Please, Raj."

He closed his eyes and tilted his head back. She could see the column of his throat move as he swallowed. "God, you're killing me," he groaned.

She pressed her lips to his breastbone, gloried in the silken feel of his skin beneath her mouth. He didn't stop her. Deliberately, she unsnapped his trousers. Pushed them down his hips until they slid the rest of the way on their own.

Finally, finally, she could cup him in her hand, nothing between them. He was so hard, like marble. So soft, like silk. She stroked him, squeezing softly.

"You win," he said on a sharp intake of breath. "You win."

And then he hooked a hand behind her knees and swept her into his arms. Carried her to the bed and lay her across it. Automatically, her legs went around his hips as he followed her down. Her body throbbed for want of him. He cupped a breast in his hand, tweaked her nipple as he kissed her again.

Then she felt him. Slowly, inexorably, he slid into her body. It burned, and she suddenly gasped with the pain of it.

He stopped moving. "Am I hurting you?"

She realized she was gripping both his biceps in her hands, her nails digging into him. Tears pressed at the back of her lids and she swallowed them down.

"It's been a long time," she said. "It's, um, more difficult than I'd thought it would be."

He swore softly. Started to withdraw.

"No," she cried out, tightening her legs around him. "I need you, Raj. I need you."

His breath sucked in, as if he were in pain, too. Which, she thought, he probably was, though it was a far different pain from what she was experiencing.

"We'll take it slowly," he said, and her heart swelled with feeling.

He put his hand between them, found her. Sweet, singing need began to hum in her body again as he stroked her. Softly, sweetly, as if he had all the time in the world. As if there was no dawn and no sunset, no appointments, no pressures. As if she was the world and he her servant within it.

It took longer to hit the peak this time, but she did, her body opening to him as he took the opportunity to slide farther inside her.

"Okay?" he asked.

"Kiss me," she said.

He did, his mouth so warm and giving that she lost herself in the kiss once more. She could feel him moving again, and though her body tightened a bit at the intrusion, the pain was far less than it had been.

She didn't know how long they lay entangled like that, but finally Veronica tilted her hips up and took him the rest of the way inside. She could feel him throbbing deep in her body, could feel the tight control he wielded over his needs as he held himself so still.

"Poor Raj," she whispered. "What a project I've turned into for you."

"You aren't a project," he said fiercely. Protectively.

She loved the conviction in his tone, loved how honorable he truly was. The feelings swirling in her heart and soul were beginning to confuse her. Frighten her. Deliberately, she shoved them away.

"Make love to me," she said.

He began to move so slowly once more, until she was a mass of tight nerve endings and shuddering tension. Until she was begging him to take her faster. He took his time obliging her, but when she didn't shrink from him, when she didn't cry out or flinch in pain, he turned up the intensity.

Again and again, he took her higher, their bodies straining together, sweating, skin sliding on skin. Exquisite. Torturous.

The pain was still there, but so slight she hardly noticed. The pleasure was far, far stronger.

And then it crested until she cried out, her entire body shuddering beneath him, wanting still more but unable to last a moment longer. His control was so exquisite, so perfect, that she knew when he gave himself permission to follow her into the abyss. He lifted her to him, his body pumping into hers one last time before he was still.

He propped himself up, careful not to crush her. In the darkness, she could still make out his features. Could see the troubled expression he couldn't mask.

"Thank you," she said, because it was all she could think to say.

"Are you all right? Did I hurt you?"

"I'm fine."

Physically, that was true. Emotionally was another story. So many emotions crashing in on her. She'd made love with him, and though she didn't regret it at all, the weight of the feelings she'd been carrying for so many months—wondering if she were damaged somehow, if she would ever feel as if she were whole again, if she would ever be able to be with a man without dissembling—was immense.

"You don't sound fine," he said. And then he rolled over and took her with him until she sprawled half on his body and half off.

"It's a bit overwhelming," she admitted.

"I get that a lot," he said smugly, and she knew he was trying to make her laugh.

It worked, damn him. "Arrogant bastard."

His fingers stroked along her spine. "Seriously," he said after a few moments. "Are you okay?"

"Yes," she said on a sigh. "I am."

It was not his finest moment. Raj lay awake long after Veronica had dozed off and contemplated the mess he'd made. What the hell had he done?

He'd never, ever slept with someone he was guarding. It had been wrong to do so, and yet he'd been powerless to resist her request.

Hell, he hadn't wanted to resist. Since the moment he'd seen her from the bar of the hotel, he'd wanted this woman with the kind of craving that abhorred him. The kind of craving that drug addicts used to justify their excesses.

That thought did not cheer him in the least.

But she'd been all gorgeous, sexy femininity, with an alluring laugh and a come-hither look that fooled every man she bestowed it upon. He'd known better than to fall for it, yet he had.

Beneath the facade, she was amazing. Serious, smart, funny and sad. Sadder than any woman he'd ever known, with the exception of his mother. He hated that sadness, wanted to take it away from her forever.

He pressed a hand to his chest. There was a dull ache there, the kind of ache he'd gotten whenever he'd come home from school to find his mother high again.

Whenever he'd been able to go to school, that is. He'd missed most of his middle school years with all the moving they'd done. How he'd ever gotten into—and graduated from—high school was as much a mystery to him as anyone.

That he was even thinking of those days right now was not a good sign.

He considered slipping from the bed and returning to the living area, where he'd been on the computer when she'd opened the window and triggered the silent alarm he'd set, but the bed was warm and she was soft and sleeping. Her head lay on his chest, her silky platinum hair a shiny tangle that he itched to shove his fingers into.

He would not move, would not risk waking her when she was sleeping so soundly—especially when she'd told him she didn't usually sleep very well.

Eventually, he fell into a light doze, his mind filled with thoughts of her—of the soft cries she'd made as he'd taken her, of the way her body opened to him, moved with him, the way she'd found her pleasure and cried out his name.

Beneath the surface, he was troubled. Troubled because she'd trusted him. She'd flat-out told him earlier that she wanted someone who would love her, who would give her a family, and though he knew he wasn't that man—couldn't ever be that man—he'd accepted her trust and taken her body because he was too weak to say no.

Because she'd gutted him with her trust and her need and he'd been powerless.

A few hours later, in the dim light of dawn, he felt her stir. Her hand slipped along his chest, her fingers spreading wide, as if she were learning him by touch. Her mouth pressed against his skin, and his body hardened instantly.

He should have gone back to his bed on the couch, but it was too late. He knew, even as her fingers found him, wrapped around him, that he was not pushing her away.

He should, he definitely should—but he couldn't. Instead, he lay there, let her stroke him, purr against his skin. He groaned her name when she climbed on top of him and took him inside her inch by slow inch.

She was so warm, so wet, and he closed his eyes, let himself feel the pleasure of her fingers splayed against his chest as she rode him slowly, so slowly he thought he would die of anticipation.

"Raj," she said. "Oh, Raj."

Once more, she broke his control. He threaded his fingers in her hair, pulled her down to him, kissed her thoroughly, his tongue sliding against hers, his lips molding hers as she began to make little noises in her throat that drove him insane.

He flipped her over, slid so deeply into her body that they both groaned with the pleasure.

"Don't stop," she said, as if sensing that he was at war with himself. "Please don't stop."

He didn't. Not for a very long time.

CHAPTER EIGHT

VERONICA woke alone. Martine stood by the bed
as usual, a maid and a breakfast tray close by.
Veronica pushed herself upright, disappointment hollowing her stomach as she blinked in
the bright morning light.

She ran her hand over Raj's side of the bed,
came away cold. He'd been gone for a long time.

Ridiculously, she thought of their fiction—
which was no longer fiction, and yet her lover
had left her. Perhaps he didn't want to be seen
with her after all.

The thought made her head throb.

Instead, she ate her breakfast, listened to
Martine detail her morning appointments and
took a shower. She dressed carefully in a bright
pink cashmere sweater dress, deciding at the
last minute to be a little naughty and pulling on
tall, suede boots to complement it.

Then she brushed her hair into a thick pony-
tail and went to face the day.

She drew up short when she entered the living area to find Brady.

And Raj, she realized. He stood by the window, looking all dark and broody and distant.

"Good morning, gentlemen," she said, her heart beginning to throb as Raj turned toward her. She couldn't tell what he was thinking. His expression was hooded, his feelings a mystery to her.

Part of her cried out in protest. How could he have made love to her the way he had and be so distant now? How could he not look at her with heat simmering in his eyes? She felt as if her feelings must be written all over her face, and yet he was as unreadable as stone.

She shot a glance at Brady. He was oblivious to the undercurrents, thank God. He walked over and gave her a hug, then took her by the hand and led her to the couch.

"You need to sit down, Veronica," he said.

The first prickles of alarm dotted her skin.

"What's going on?" Her gaze slewed from Brady to Raj.

"I'm sorry, Veronica," Raj said, his sexy voice so impartial and cool. Not at all the voice of the man who'd whispered in her ear last night. Who'd told her she was beautiful and amazing as he'd thrust deep inside her.

Her heart squeezed tight at the memory. She wanted that man back, the one who was tender and loving and worshipped her body so beautifully that he'd given her back something of herself. He'd made her feel as if she deserved to be treated special. As if, for a short while, she wasn't a horrible woman who'd lost her child because she'd been careless.

He'd made her feel whole.

"There's been a coup in Aliz," he continued. "The chief of police has seized all the government buildings in the capital. He's calling for your ouster and the restoration of the former president."

"He can't do that," she said numbly. But he could. He had. She rose, her limbs shaking with sudden fury. "I won't let him."

"Sweetie," Brady said, but she held her hand up to silence him.

Raj, however, did not remain silent.

"I know what you're thinking. But it's too dangerous for you to return. You need to remain here."

"And do what?" she demanded, fury swirling inside. "Do nothing?" She shook her head. "I can't sit by and let them get away with this. I won't."

Raj's eyes flashed. "They won't get away with

it," he said. "But it'll take time to sort it out. In the meantime, you're in danger, especially if you try to return to Aliz."

But he didn't know her country, didn't know her responsibility. She wasn't backing down, wasn't abandoning the people who had elected her. She couldn't.

"I'm returning to Aliz," she said. "With or without you."

"Very well," he said. So cool, so casual. Even when he lost the battle, he appeared to be in complete control. It irritated her.

"Just like that?" she said. "No arguing? No attempts to persuade me otherwise?"

He inclined his head. "Just like that." Then he turned and walked toward the door.

Her chest ached at the thought he was leaving her after what they'd been through together. So easily, as if it meant nothing.

Which it probably hadn't. He'd told her he couldn't give her anything else. It was her fault if she wanted to believe more was possible.

"You aren't just going to leave her, are you?" Brady called out angrily.

Raj stopped and turned back to them, hand on the door. "No. I'm going to pack."

Three hours later, they were airborne. Veronica sat in a plush leather seat and gazed out at the snowy English landscape below. She knew she owed the speed of their departure to Raj.

Without him, she'd still be waiting on a chartered plane since Aliz did not maintain a government fleet. Instead, Raj had let her use one of VSI's company jets. She and her staff were on their way home, thanks to him.

He sat across the aisle from her, engrossed in whatever was on his computer screen at the moment. He'd barely said a word to her in the three hours since he'd come into her suite and told her of the situation in Aliz.

She'd been mortified to have to hear it from him when she should have known before he did.

Yet another sign that Raj was powerful and connected.

His fingers tapped something on the keys, and a current of heat swirled in her belly. Those fingers had touched her so expertly, had drawn such need and passion from her that thinking of it now made her wet. She wanted him again, in spite of everything.

He must have sensed something, because he looked up at that moment, his gaze turning swiftly to capture hers. She didn't bother to pretend she hadn't been staring. Her heart skipped a beat. Her nipples began to tighten against the cashmere of her sweater dress.

His gaze slid down, then back up again, his eyes glittering with heat and need that mirrored her own. A thrill shot through her. He still wanted her. Maybe one night hadn't been enough.

It was impossible, though. There was a bed on this plane, but there was no way they could retreat to it. Between her staff, his team and the flight crew, there was no hope of privacy.

And once they reached Aliz, who knew what would happen?

He snapped his computer closed and pushed up from his seat. Then he was sinking into the seat beside hers, and her skin was prickling with his nearness. Her blood was singing with heat and need.

She picked up the vodka cocktail the flight attendant had brought to her—she'd hoped it would calm her nerves—and took a small sip. The vodka wasn't strong, but it kicked back nevertheless, burning her throat in a good way.

"Thank you," she said.

"You've already thanked me at least fifty times," he replied, his voice low and containing an edge she didn't quite recognize. "I couldn't let you go alone. They would devour you in a matter of minutes."

She met his gaze, her heart turning over at

the intense look in those golden eyes. "Maybe I was thanking you for last night."

He didn't say anything for a long moment. "Just when I think you can't get to me," he said, shaking his head.

"I get to you?" For some reason, that made her stomach leap.

"In the worst way," he replied seriously.

Veronica frowned. "I'm not sure that's very flattering."

He picked up her hand where it rested on her lap, threaded his fingers through hers. Her pulse shot into overdrive. Her core throbbed with need for him, her body tightening painfully. When he lifted her fingers to his lips and kissed them, a shiver rocketed through her.

"Raj…"

"I want to spread you out on silken sheets, Veronica," he said, his voice pitched for her ears alone. "I want to lick you everywhere, kiss you, thrust into your body."

She closed her eyes. "I can't take this. Don't talk to me like this."

"I want to take you hard, soft, slow, fast. I want to take you often. And I want you to wear those damn thigh-high boots you've got on while I do it."

Veronica was drowning in need and frustration. "Stop," she choked out. A few rows away, Martine looked up at Veronica's cry, met her gaze. Just as quickly she turned away again, a red flush spreading across her cheeks.

Veronica wanted to tell Martine it was okay, but she couldn't speak. Because at the moment Raj drew one of her fingers into his mouth, sucked it in and out so slowly as fingers of fire raced along her nerve endings. She bit her lip to stop a moan. He kissed her palm, then leaned forward and took her mouth in a hard, sensual kiss.

She didn't care who saw them. She cupped his jaw, kissed him back with all the passion and fire he aroused in her. If they were alone, she'd have him undressed and inside her before the next few moments passed.

"Now what do you think?" he whispered in her ear. "Flattered or not?"

"Yes," she breathed, heart racing. Martine was engrossed in a magazine now, and Veronica took another sip of her cocktail while Raj leaned back on the seat and shot her the most sexy grin imaginable.

"I'm hard for you," he said. "Another minute of that and I'd be lifting that Barbie-doll-pink dress and to hell with everyone else."

"Another minute of that and I'd let you," she

replied. And then she laughed. "Barbie-doll pink? How do you know that, Raj?"

"How else? Barbie was my favorite doll," he said—and then he winked as she gaped at him.

"You say things like that just to make me laugh."

He shrugged. "Sometimes." Then he picked up her hand again, threaded their fingers together. "My mom moved us around a lot when I was growing up. One of the things I remember, when I was about eight I think, was this little girl in my class. She was blonde, like you, and she had these enormous pigtails. She was the prettiest thing I'd ever seen, and she carried a pink backpack with a Barbie face on it."

"You must have liked her."

"I did."

She thought of him as a love-struck little boy and smiled. "So what happened? Did you write one of those notes to her where you asked her to circle 'yes' or 'no'?" she teased.

"No. But she did invite me to her birthday party. I remember the invitation was pink, with Barbie dolls on it."

"Was the party pink-themed, too?"

"I don't know," he said. "I never got to go. We moved again."

She imagined the disappointment he must

have felt when he couldn't go to the party. "I'm sorry you didn't get to go."

"I probably wouldn't have liked it anyway. There'd have been a pink cake, no doubt, and pink balloons everywhere. And what if I'd been the only boy invited?" He gave a mock shudder.

"The horrors," she agreed. And then she sighed. "At least you got to go places. I never did."

She thought of her vast bedroom with the purple walls, the piles of toys and the utter loneliness that had so often assailed her. She'd had a nanny, but even Mrs. Petit couldn't completely fill the emptiness created by the vacuum her father had placed her in. A vacuum made all the worse by the fact they'd had a normal life until her mother had died in the accident.

Veronica had spent the past several years of her life trying to fill that emptiness; it'd gotten her nothing but heartbreak.

"One thing I've learned in this life," he said, "is that the grass always looks greener on the other side of the fence—though it usually isn't."

"Maybe so," she said. "But sometimes it just might be."

"It does no good to think like that, Veronica. It only leads to regrets. And they might be false regrets."

She turned to look out the window. They were over water now, winging their way toward the island of Aliz in the Mediterranean. "I have enough regrets to last me a lifetime."

She could feel the weight of his stare on her, but she didn't turn. Tears were suddenly pressing against the backs of her eyes. Stupid, stupid tears. If she looked at him, she wasn't sure she could stop them from falling.

But why? What was it about him that made her want to unburden her soul to him every damn time?

She sucked in a breath, nibbled on her thumbnail. So quickly, she'd grown to trust him. So quickly, she'd grown to care about him. And she still knew next to nothing about him.

"You can cry if you need to," he said, so softly that she almost didn't hear.

How did he know? She turned to face him again, resolutely burying the tears and forcing herself to smile.

"Not at all," she replied. "I was just thinking."

He didn't look convinced. "It's a long trip, Veronica," he finally said. "Why don't you rest?"

"Nonsense. It's only a couple more hours. And we really should discuss what happens when we arrive." She had to concentrate on that, on the moment the plane landed and she set foot on her home soil again. She'd only been gone two weeks, and she'd set in motion much that would be ruined if she didn't quickly get this situation under control.

Giancarlo Zarella would never agree to build a resort in Aliz if they couldn't maintain the rule of law.

Raj's eyes sparked. "There's nothing to discuss," he said. "I'll handle it."

Veronica blinked. "You'll handle it? Handle what? I think we should at least discuss the possibilities."

"No," he said, his voice harder than it had been only moments ago.

A current of anger swirled in her belly. "No? I'm not a child, Raj. I have a right to know what your plans are."

He got to his feet, every inch the imperious lord and master. Then he shoved a hand through his hair—and she realized that he looked as if he hadn't slept much lately.

Her fault, no doubt.

"We'll discuss it before we arrive," he said.

Veronica bit down on the spike of temper. Perhaps he was still finalizing his plans and didn't want to share them yet. Or maybe he had no idea what to expect when they arrived. She could wait another hour. She'd trusted him this far, and he hadn't failed her yet.

"Fine. But I expect a full report quite soon."

His mouth was a hard line. "You'll get it, believe me."

Veronica awoke with a start, confusion crashing through her. Then she remembered that she was on a plane, flying back to Aliz. After Raj had walked away, she'd closed her eyes for a few minutes. She hadn't expected to fall so soundly asleep.

Or maybe she had, considering how little sleep she'd gotten the night before. A flight attendant materialized at that moment. "Madam President, would you like something to eat?"

She started to refuse, then realized her stomach was growling. But they would be in Aliz soon, and she could wait. She sent the man away with a request for water instead and turned to raise the window covering that someone had lowered.

Her blood froze as myriad stars glittered against a sea of black. It was wrong, all wrong. It shouldn't be dark yet. Aliz was only four hours from the U.K., and they'd left early enough to arrive before nightfall.

Veronica unsnapped her seat belt. Before

she could rise, Raj was there. His hands were shoved in the pockets of his camel trousers. His navy shirt was unbuttoned partway, exposing a tanned V of skin, and his dark hair curled over the collar, so carefree and sexy, as if he belonged on a beach instead of here.

Her heart beat sharply. "Where are we, Raj? Where are you taking us?"

Part of her already knew she'd been betrayed, but the other part—the part that had trusted this man with her body and soul last night, that still wanted to trust him—refused to believe he could be so duplicitous. It was a mistake, that's all. She'd simply miscalculated, or they'd had to go a different route for some reason.

There was no way he was forcing his wishes upon her. No way he was taking her somewhere against her will. He wouldn't do that.

"We're going to my home in Goa," he said, and her stomach went into a free fall.

She was stunned, as if she'd been running fast and suddenly smacked up against a brick wall.

"Goa? Isn't that a bit far from Aliz?" She sounded so bitter, so terribly bitter. Fury was bubbling in her veins like a volcano preparing to erupt—she felt as if she would burst apart at the seams if she had to stay on this plane a moment longer.

But what choice did she have? What goddamn choice?

He had her right where he wanted her—and he was *controlling* her, taking away her autonomy, locking her up. Revulsion mixed into the vile stew inside her, rose into her throat so that she wanted to retch with the bitterness of it.

She would not do so. She would not crumble, not now.

"I'm sorry, Veronica," he said, though he didn't look sorry at all. "But it's necessary. You can't go back to Aliz just yet because it's not safe for you there. The chief of police controls the government—and all the weapons, I might add. If we landed, he could execute you—all of us—before the next sunrise."

She was a block of ice. Her teeth began to chatter, though she tried very hard not to let them. It was no use. Raj swore, sinking down into the seat beside her and gathering her into his arms before she could stop him.

He was so warm, so solid. And she wanted to melt against him, wanted him to hold her while she thawed, while she drew his heat into her body.

But she couldn't. She couldn't accept comfort from him when he'd betrayed her. She'd trusted him, given him something of herself that she'd been unable to give in a very long time, and it meant nothing to him. He'd betrayed her so easily.

Veronica shoved him as hard as she could. "No," she said between clenched teeth. "Let me go. I *hate* you."

"I'm sorry," he said again, his grip not loosening. "I had to do it. I won't let them harm you."

An angry sob tore from her throat before she could stop it. And then she was fighting like a madwoman, shoving hard, screaming her fury. He let her go and she scrambled back, away from him, pressing herself against the wall, her knees drawing up to fend him off if he tried to touch her again.

He did not do so.

His gaze was troubled, but unrepentant. There was a long red scratch down his cheek, but she refused to care. If it hurt, so much the better. He deserved it.

"How dare you?" she snapped. "How dare you think you have the right to decide *for* me?"

His eyes flashed, and then his expression hardened. "Go ahead and have your tantrum, Veronica, but would you put them in danger, too?" he asked coldly, jerking his head toward the rear of the cabin and the men and women who sat there, pretending not to stare at them.

"You have no idea what that man is willing to do, no idea what awaits you—or them—and yet you would have me take you there? You might risk it on your behalf, but can you risk it on theirs?"

She hated that he made her feel guilty, hated that he sounded sensible. Hated that he turned this against her when he was the one who'd betrayed *her*. She drew in a shaky breath, trying so damn hard not to cry—because she was furious, damn it, not because she was weak—and glared at him.

"No one would hurt them," she said. "They've done nothing wrong. I'm the only one who need fear reprisal."

"You don't know that," he said, his words measured. "You only think you do."

Then he stood and looked down at her, his presence so big and imposing and infuriating. She wanted to tear his eyes out.

And she wanted to kiss him. The force of the longing took her breath away.

Veronica closed her eyes and turned her head, her cheek pressing against the cold, vibrating wall of the airplane cabin. *No, never again.* Her body might not realize that everything had changed, but she did. She could never, ever trust him again.

"Go away," she said. "I don't want to talk to you."

She didn't think he would go, but when she cracked open an eye after a long silence, he was gone.

And she felt emptier than ever.

CHAPTER NINE

IT WAS early morning when they landed at Dabolim Airport on the Bay of Dona Paula. The aquamarine water sparkled like fire-tipped diamonds in the morning sunlight as the plane came in for a landing. After the snow in the U.K., the blinding blue sky was insufferably cheerful.

Veronica didn't feel in the least bit happy, however, though the sky was clear and the landscape looked impossibly green and verdant and warm.

She had changed into something a bit more suited to the weather in Goa—a tangerine silk sheath and a pair of nude peep-toe pumps, since she'd not packed sandals for her official trip across the mostly chilly United States and Europe.

When the cabin door opened and she stepped out onto the stairs, the heat and humidity wrapped around her senses and eased the chill in her bones. It was certainly welcome after wintry London, but Aliz would have been warm as well—not quite this warm, but not as frigid as northern Europe, either.

There was no press awaiting them, which was both a surprise and a relief. She felt far too off balance just now to deal with the media hounding her. Somehow, Raj must have managed to keep their destination a secret. How long he could do so was another matter altogether.

Martine was beside her as they descended the stairs. Georges was behind them, and the rest of the staff followed. In spite of the situation, she held her head high, determined to maintain the dignity of her office. For their sakes as well as her own.

She'd spoken with them last night, after she'd managed to regain some of her balance, and been surprised that no one seemed to disagree with Raj's plan. The security staff had understandably been dismayed at the turn of events both in Aliz and in London—when they'd climbed aboard Raj's plane and put themselves at his mercy—but somehow he'd won them over in spite of it. Now they were content to let him run the show.

She was not. She was furiously, murderously angry.

Ahead of them, Raj stood near a fleet of Land
Rovers, talking with one of the drivers. He'd
changed into a pair of khaki pants, sandals and
a dark T-shirt that stretched over the hard muscles of his biceps and chest, delineating every
line and bulge. Her heart throbbed painfully, her
body tightening in response.

She hated that she couldn't stop her reaction to
him. She wanted to smother it, and bury it down
deep. Instead, the slight soreness between her
legs reminded her of all they'd done together,
of the silken slide of his body within hers. The
driving pleasure. The bliss of orgasm.

Stop.

His betrayal, coming so hard on the heels of
their intimacy, stung all the more. She'd *trusted*
him—and he'd shattered that trust into a million shards.

He looked up then, his eyes shaded behind
mirrored sunglasses. Though she couldn't see
them, she knew he was looking directly at her.
Her body sizzled under his regard, her nipples
tingling, her core flooding with heat.

Damn him!

He separated himself from the driver and
came to her side. Martine fell back, out of ear-
shot. Veronica wanted to turn and tell her secretary there was no need, but she refused to do

so lest Raj think she couldn't handle him on her own.

"How are you this morning?" he asked.

A riot of emotions tore through her at the silken sound of his voice. She hardened her heart and kept looking straight ahead. "Furious," she spluttered.

"But alive," he added, and she whipped her head sideways to glare at him. The red mark on his face was fading. She hadn't drawn blood, so it would disappear soon. She wanted to reach out and touch him, soothe him—and she wanted to mark him again. The feelings warring inside her were so tangled that it hurt to try and sort them all out.

"You say that like you know for certain what would have happened in Aliz. You don't, so I would appreciate it if you would admit there were other possibilities."

He shrugged, further inflaming her. "It's possible. But what I do is plan for the worst—and then avoid it."

"Or perhaps you create the worst," she said. "Aliz had a chance before you abducted me. Now, no one will come to her rescue."

She didn't truly know that, but she was too angry not to say it.

His frown turned down the corners of his sensual mouth. "And who is making assumptions now? I hardly think it's my actions you need worry about. It's Monsieur Brun's and the chief of police's."

Her heart skipped a beat at the former president's name. He had not liked her, that was certain. He'd attacked her in the media for months before the election, and he'd said the most vile things. That, however, was politics.

"Have you had more news?"

"None yet. The police have shut down communications for the time being. Nothing is getting out now."

She could hope that somehow Signor Zarella remained ignorant of the situation, though she didn't count on having that kind of good fortune. News of the coup had already made it to CNN, and it was only a matter of time before more news started to trickle out of Aliz again.

"I should be there," she said.

"You should be anywhere *but* there," Raj replied.

They'd reached one of the Land Rovers. He opened the door for her and she climbed in. When he got in beside her, she turned away from him, her pulse kicking up at his nearness. Martine and the others settled into the other cars, and then they were on their way, rolling south through lush country filled with palm trees, tall grasses and jade-green rice paddies. In the distance, gray shadowed hills rose up as a backdrop to the lush landscape.

It was exotic and beautiful, as were the brightly colored saris of the women they passed on the road. Goa was a mixture of the modern and ancient, and she found herself studying everything with the kind of interest of someone who'd always longed to go places. She'd traveled plenty over the past ten years, but she'd never come to India...an oversight she was sorry for now that she was here.

They passed the crumbled ruins of something that looked like a medieval fortress, and she craned her head as it faded away behind them again. It had seemed so odd, so strangely European in this setting.

"The Portuguese settled in Goa in the sixteenth century," Raj said, correctly guessing at her thoughts. "They only recently left. Much of their architecture is still evident in the villages and towns. Their influence can be found in the food, and there are even a few churches that remain."

She didn't want to look at him, but she did anyway. "You are originally from here?"

His expression seemed distant, a bit sad perhaps. "My father was Goan, though I did not know him. He and my mother divorced when I was two."

"But you have a house here."

"Yes. I wanted to see my heritage, or half of it anyway."

"Do you have family nearby?"

"If I do, I don't know them. My father died in England when I was a child. Any connection to family was lost a long time ago."

"Where does your mother live, then?" She didn't want to talk to him, and yet she couldn't seem to stop herself. She remembered that his mother was American, and she was curious. He seemed so exotic, as if he belonged here, and yet he was actually more American, or European, than he was Indian.

"She's in a home," he said, his eyes so distant and troubled. "Her mind is gone now. She doesn't know who I am."

In spite of her anger, a swell of emotion threatened to clog her throat. "I'm sorry, Raj. That must be terrible for you."

"She did it to herself," he said. "Drug use."

He said the words so matter-of-factly, but she knew they hurt him. She could see it in his expression, in the way he stared into the distance, as if he didn't see her beside him. What must he have suffered, watching his mother go through something like that?

She didn't remember her mother. She had impressions sometimes of a soft, laughing woman that were so fleeting she wondered if she'd imagined them. Her father had never talked of her mother once she was gone. He'd simply smothered his daughter in an attempt to keep her from leaving him, too. As if death could be cheated by imprisonment.

They rode the rest of the way in silence, finally turning and climbing steadily up a hill until they reached a sprawling estate that perched over the Arabian Sea below. The land was dotted with tall swaying palms, green grass that tumbled down to white-sand beaches and bordered by the sparkling sea that went on forever before finally curving into the horizon.

It was beautiful, far more beautiful than she'd realized it would be. The sea view reminded her of Aliz, and a pang of emotion clawed into her belly as she thought of her nation. What was happening there now? Would she ever see her home again?

A woman in a bright turquoise sari edged in gold and shot through with green threads emerged from the house, followed by a cadre of servants, who collected luggage and issued instructions. Veronica's gaze kept straying to the sea, and when she finally looked back again, she realized that she and Raj were alone.

"The view is even better from the terrace," he said.

"Where is my staff?"

"They've been shown to the guest cottages. Don't worry, they will be quite comfortable there."

"I'd like a guest cottage, too," she said, her heart suddenly picking up speed again at the prospect of being left alone with him.

"You will stay in the main house," he said. "With me."

"I'd rather not." She lifted her hand to shade her eyes as he moved, the light off his sunglasses reflecting the sun and sending a bright shaft of light into her vision.

Then he was before her, so close—too close— and the brightness was gone.

"You have no choice," he replied. "It is for your safety."

A shiver of dread washed over her. And then there was something else. Something warm and electric. Something he caused by standing so near, by filling her senses with his scent and his presence.

"And who will keep me safe from you?" she said softly.

One corner of his mouth lifted in a faint smile. A predatory smile. "That is entirely up to you, Veronica. I won't touch you unless you ask me to."

"I won't," she declared. "I'd rather curl up with a cobra."

He laughed. "This is India. That can be arranged."

Veronica followed him into the house, the brightly clad woman appearing once more as soon as they were inside. She spoke to Raj in a language Veronica didn't recognize. He said something in return, slowly she thought, as if he were figuring out the words.

And then the woman was turning and sweeping down the hallway like a dazzling exotic bird flying away.

"Your room is this way," he said, leading her down a hall to a polished wooden door. Iron hinges and studs decorated the edges, and carvings of elephants, tigers and flowers marched in profusion across the surface.

Raj opened the door without seeming to notice its beauty and held it for her. She preceded him inside, and found her luggage already waiting at the end of the bed. Double doors were open to the outside, leading onto a terrace. She went out, drawn once more by the sea view. She hadn't realized how tense she'd been over the past few weeks, but something about this place calmed her. In spite of her fear and anger, she felt strangely calm beneath all the emotion.

A breeze lifted her hair, blew it across her face. She pushed the strands down again and breathed deeply. She wasn't precisely free here, but at least he hadn't shut her into a room with four walls, tiny windows and one door. She could come and go as she pleased, though she didn't fool herself that she wouldn't be watched or that she could leave this estate and keep on going right back to the airport and thence to Aliz.

She wasn't that free.

She didn't have to turn to know he was standing behind her. The hair on her arms had prickled as he drew near. Even now, her body was zinging with electric sparks. Longing was a palpable force within her.

If only she were here under different circumstances. If only. The story of her life, really.

She had merely to lean back, and she would connect with his solid form. He would put his arms around her as she tilted her head to the side, gave him access to her neck. His mouth would skim along her throat, her shoulder, and then he would turn her in his arms and kiss her.

She closed her eyes, her chin dropping as the weight of her need pressed down on her. And the weight of her sadness.

"You should have consulted me," she said bitterly. "You should have treated me like I was capable of offering an intelligent opinion on the subject. Bringing me here against my will was wrong."

He sighed. "You left me no choice. You were determined to go to Aliz, no matter what anyone said to you."

"It was my choice to make, not yours."

"We will never agree on this subject, Veronica."

She turned then, taking a step back. He regarded her with golden eyes that made her heart skip. So beautiful. So exotic. He'd always been exotic, and yet this setting made him more so.

"What happens now, Raj? I'm here with you, but I still have a responsibility to the people of Aliz. I can't simply give up."

"You aren't giving up. Your people have issued statements on your behalf. World pressure will be brought to bear on Monsieur Brun."

She blew out a breath. "I don't like waiting," she said. "I've never been very good at it."

He reached out, lifted a tendril of her hair,

rubbed it between his thumb and forefinger. "I can wait," he said, his voice a deep, sensual growl that vibrated into her belly. "I can wait as long as it takes. Sometimes, the reward is much sweeter after the waiting."

Every cell in her body was attuned to him. Her breath had stilled, her heart, her blood—everything silent, waiting…waiting for a touch that never came.

He dropped her hair, stepped back. "Dinner is at six," he said. "Wear something simple—but stunning."

"Why?" she asked, the pulse point between her legs throbbing now. "Will there be guests?"

"Perhaps." And then he left her alone on the terrace, the breeze gently caressing her, tormenting her. If she closed her eyes, she could almost imagine the tendrils of wind were his fingers, skimming oh so lightly along her skin.

At precisely six o'clock, Veronica emerged from her room, dressed in a simple black gown that was strapless and long, skimming her form down to her ankles. One side was slit to her thigh, and she'd chosen to wear tall crimson heels with jeweled straps. For jewelry, she'd kept it simple. A diamond pendant and earrings, a lone diamond bracelet.

She hadn't heard any cars arrive, but she'd napped until nearly five-thirty before she'd awakened with a start and hurriedly gotten dressed. Now, as she glided through the sprawling house, following her nose toward the delicious scents of curry and spice, she realized there was no sound except the occasional distant voice speaking in Konkani.

The dining room was empty, but a long wall of wooden doors was opened to the terrace. She stepped out, expecting to find a small gathering of people. Perhaps Raj had invited powerful friends who could somehow help her.

But there was no one. Nothing except a long wooden table set for two with hibiscus blossoms and gleaming crystal, china and silverware. Torches flickered around the perimeter and the sound of the sea washing the beach drifted up from below. A lone man stood at one end of the terrace. She knew who it was even before he turned.

Her heart caught at the sight of him in an ornate green silk *sherwani* coat over traditional trousers. His dark hair had been cut since she'd last seen him this morning, the ends no longer curling over his collar. He looked like a maharaja, so exotic and handsome and regal that he took her breath away.

"Where is everyone?" she asked, because she could think of nothing else to say.

He came forward and poured a glass of wine for her. She accepted it, her body reacting with a shiver as his fingers brushed against hers ever so lightly.

"It's just us tonight," he said, his voice wrapping around her senses, caressing them.

"My staff?"

"Dinner in their cottages, I assume."

She'd met with them earlier when she'd spent part of the afternoon making phone calls about the situation in Aliz. They were all tired, all stressed by what had happened. And perhaps a bit regretful that they'd been with her in London. If they'd been at home in Aliz, they'd be swept into this change from the inside and simply riding the wave until it came to rest onshore. But because they were with her, they were now outsiders, too.

Veronica took a sip of the wine, frustration and guilt hammering through her.

"Don't beat yourself up, Veronica," Raj said gently.

"What makes you think I was doing so?"

He shrugged, his golden eyes gleaming in the torchlight. "Call it a hunch."

"Is anyone else coming?" she asked, and then

felt stupid since he'd just informed her it would only be the two of them.

"No," he said, the corners of his mouth lifting in a faint smile.

He pulled a chair out for her and then sat in another nearby. At that moment, a waiter came outside with a tray. There were many small silver dishes containing food in red sauces, green sauces and bright amber sauces. There was also creamy *raita* and naan bread, as well as fragrant basmati rice. Fried fish, fried prawns and salads of purple onion slices with tomatoes and cucumber rounded out the variety. And then there was chutney and thin, crispy yellow *papadum*.

If she weren't so hungry, she'd get up and go back to her room. She was supposed to be angry with him, not companionable. But the food smelled too good, and the night air was warm and fresh.

And she just didn't feel like fighting with him again after the stress of the past twenty-four hours.

"Fish curry is a Goan specialty," he said after she'd filled her plate with a bit of everything.

She took a bite and the flavors exploded on her tongue—the spice, the fresh fish, the tomatoes and hints of coconut milk. "It's delicious," she said.

It was awkward at first, but eventually they started to talk about subjects that weren't sensitive in the least. They avoided anything personal, avoided Aliz or what had happened between them last night. There was even a discussion of Bollywood movies—Raj hadn't seen many, and Veronica was surprised.

"I was born in Britain, but raised in America," he explained. "And then I joined the military. I haven't spent a lot of time watching any movies, much less Indian ones."

"How did you like the military?" she asked, dipping a piece of naan into a masala sauce before popping it into her mouth.

He didn't look at her. "Well enough," he said. "It got me where I am today."

She could picture him in military fatigues, silver dog tags hanging from a chain around his neck. He was tall, broad, tough—the kind of man to whom a weapon was an extension of his body and not just a foreign object. It's what made him so good, she realized. And so lonely.

"So where is home for you? Where is the place you most identify with?"

She wasn't sure, but it seemed as if he stiffened. And then he was looking at her sharply before he smoothed his expression. "I'm a mutt," he said. "I have no specific home."

"A mutt?"

"Someone of mixed ancestry, like a dog that you can't quite tell what the dominant breed is."

"But you live in London," she said, trying to approach it from a different angle. "Is that the place you prefer over the rest?"

"I don't prefer anywhere. I go where I want to go."

"Like here?"

"Precisely."

She took another sip of wine. "But what about when you're ready for a family? Where will you settle then?"

His eyes were hard, glittering. "Don't, Veronica," he said. "Don't take this conversation down that road."

She tilted her chin up to glare at him icily, though her stomach was doing flips. "Don't flatter yourself. I was simply making conversation, not trying to set up house with you."

He shoved a hand through his hair and leaned back on his chair. The torches crackled, the sea churned, and he was silent for a long moment. "It's complicated," he finally said. "I'm complicated."

"Aren't we all." She said it as a statement, not a question, and he looked at her, appraising her.

"You certainly are," he said softly. And then

he took a drink of his wine. "Family is not for me," he said. "It's not what I want."

Her heart pinched in her chest. Yes, she did want a family—a husband, children—but she didn't want them right this moment. Nor was she naive enough to think that one night of sex with Raj made him her ideal man, her love for all time. But the fact he could state so emphatically that a family was out of the question…

Yes, it bothered her. Because it seemed as if men never thought of her in terms of family life. They thought of her for sex. For uncomplicated, uncommitted relationships based on physical attraction.

There was nothing deeper. There never had been. And that saddened her.

She set her napkin on the table, pushed back and got to her feet. "Thank you for a wonderful meal," she said. "But I think I've had enough excitement for one day. It's time to turn in."

"Veronica," he said, standing, holding his hand out as if to stop her.

She turned slightly, her gaze not on him but on a point behind him. "It's okay, Raj," she said. "I understand. I'm just tired."

"It has nothing to do with you. I just don't feel the need for those things. I'm happy the way I am."

"Are you?" she said, her voice stiff even though she tried to make it casual.

He looked as if he pitied her. She hated it, because she knew what he was thinking. It made her wish she'd never told him about the baby. She didn't want his pity. She didn't want anyone's pity. She didn't deserve it.

"Not everyone needs the same things out of life. I have money and freedom. I need nothing more."

"How lonely that sounds," she said. "And what happens in twenty years when you wake up and realize you have no one who cares?"

He shook his head slowly. "You'll find him, Veronica."

"Find who?" she asked, quaking inside.

He reached out and skimmed a finger along her cheek. "The man who will love you the way you want to be loved."

CHAPTER TEN

HE SHOULD have left her alone, should have let her nurture her anger with him and left it at that. He shouldn't have planned to have dinner with her, shouldn't have asked her to dress up for him, and shouldn't have sat for more than an hour talking with her about anything and everything, listening to her bright laughter and falling just a little more under her spell with every word.

Raj shook his head as he stood on the terrace and let the wind whip through his clothes. It was hot and humid, but the breeze took it all away, for a short time anyway.

Why couldn't he simply leave well enough alone? He'd hurt her when he'd taken her body, and he'd hurt her when he'd betrayed her trust and brought her to Goa against her will. Tonight, he'd hurt her again when he'd been unwilling to tell her why he didn't feel at home anywhere, why he couldn't settle into a family life.

Things with Veronica had gotten out of control much too quickly. He'd broken his own code of conduct when he'd gotten involved with her, and he was willing to break it again for one more night in her arms. The truth was that he'd sell his soul for one more night with her.

He wasn't proud of it, but there it was.

She wasn't like other women. He'd had relationships, some lasting for several months as he'd stayed put in one location or another, but he'd never felt as if his skin was itching on the inside, as if only one woman could soothe the restlessness that plagued him.

It was simply the circumstances of their meeting, he told himself. He'd expected a spoiled, useless brat who'd somehow fooled an entire nation—but he'd found a thoughtful, intelligent woman who hadn't led a perfect life, but who wanted very much to do a perfect job.

He admired that. Admired her. Two days ago, he'd have never thought that possible.

She'd experienced great sorrow in her life, but she hadn't let it beat her down. Her spirit was unbroken, though perhaps sorely tested.

She'd trusted him, in more ways than one, and he'd broken that trust. He didn't like the way that made him feel.

With a curse, Raj strode into the house and to her bedroom door. She'd only been gone for a half an hour or so. She might be in bed, but he would bet she was still awake. He knocked softly.

When she didn't answer, he knocked again, more loudly. Still nothing.

His heart kicked up. There was nowhere she could go really. They weren't on an island, but there was nothing for miles—and he did have security on the perimeter. He'd given her the illusion of complete freedom, but he wasn't so incautious as to leave her unguarded.

Even here.

With a curse, he pushed on the handle...and the door swung inward. The doors to the terrace were wide-open, the white curtains blowing in the breeze. She wasn't in bed, or in the en suite bath. He slipped out onto the terrace—a different terrace than the one they'd had dinner on, facing a different direction—but she wasn't there, either.

She was still on the premises, or security would have alerted him. He eyed the path that sloped down to the beach and knew instinctively where she'd gone.

Heart lodging in his throat, he took the path at a run and skidded down the hill. Veronica was not so stupid as to try and escape, was she? Because though she wouldn't get away, she might very well harm herself in the process.

And he couldn't stand it if anything happened to her.

At the bottom of the hill, the path abruptly ended in sand. He stood, looking in both directions, his ears straining to hear anything over the sound of the sea caressing the shore. A flash of something caught his eye and he took off in that direction.

He was only a few feet away when he heard singing, and he crashed to a halt. Relief flooded him as she turned her head, the moonlight catching her blond hair.

"Veronica," he said, and the singing stopped.

"I couldn't sleep." She turned to face him, her pale arms wrapped around her chest. "How about you?"

He wanted to laugh in agreement, and he wanted to snatch her into his arms and hold her tight. "You're still in your evening gown," he said, noticing with a jolt the way her creamy thigh split through the fabric as she took a step forward. Her feet were bare, her legs so long and perfect. He could still feel them wrapped around his waist, could feel how they'd trembled and stiffened when he'd brought her to orgasm.

He wanted that again.

"It doesn't matter," she said.

"I'm sorry." It was the thing he'd wanted to say, the reason he'd gone to her room in the first place.

"For what, Raj?" Her voice sounded tremulous, as if she were trying very hard not to allow any emotion to escape.

"For everything," he said. "For bringing you here. For making love to you—"

She laughed, the sound bitter. "Of course," she said, "of course. Because it would be better if you had not done so, correct? I corrupted you, corrupted your squeaky-clean morals—"

"Stop it," he said harshly. "I made love to you because I wanted to. But I shouldn't have been so weak. I should have resisted."

"Yes, of course." She turned toward the sea again, but he could see the lone tear that slid down her cheek. "I'm not the sort of woman a man resists, am I? But I am the sort he regrets."

"I don't regret it," he growled. But he did. He regretted that he'd been so weak in the first place, that he'd been unable to resist and that he'd hurt her in the process.

"Don't bother explaining," she said. "I understand."

He reached for her, his fingers closing around her bare arm. She was delicate, like spun glass in his hand. He feared that if he held her too tightly, she'd break.

"You understand nothing," he said, turning her to face him. He was careful not to pull her closer, though he wanted to.

"Oh, Raj," she said, her voice carrying to him on the sea-scented breeze, "I'm not sure either one of us understand."

"Then tell me what I need to know," he replied. Because he very much wanted to know what made her tick. There was the baby, her loss—and yet there was more. He wanted to know everything, though a small voice told him it wasn't a good idea.

The less he knew, the better in the end.

Her hand came up, her fingers sliding along his jaw. Her touch was like fire, like ice. She burned him, and he wanted nothing more than to keep burning.

"I'm so angry with you," she said, "and yet I can't help but want you, too. Why is that? Why can't I resist you?"

Her admission sent a current of hot possessiveness through him. His body hardened. He turned his head, kissed her palm. She did not pull away. Her sky-blue eyes sparkled in the night, diamond-tipped with tears.

He had done that to her. But no matter how

much he wanted her just now, he couldn't make her cry again. Because she would. He would walk away in the end, and she would cry.

And he didn't want that. Somehow, he had to find the strength to let her go.

Before this got any more complicated than it already was.

"I only want what's best for you, Veronica," he said. "If I had let you go to Aliz and something happened, I would never forgive myself."

Her laugh was strangled. "My God, you sound just like my father." Her hand dropped and her head tilted back. Her gaze sparkled up at him. "He kept me locked up until I was eighteen, until I was old enough to leave home and do what I wanted to do. His excuse was that he loved me. And he did, I know that. But it was horrible, Raj, horrible to be kept prisoner to someone else's fears for so long."

So much about her made sense now. Her wild life, her rebellion, her refusal to take a backseat while someone else steered the cart. She wanted a say because she was frightened of giving up control. He could understand that. Could empathize with it. He thought of her last night, on the plane, and felt guilty.

"This isn't the same," he said gently—justifying his actions, yes, but also because it was true. "There is a real threat to your safety, especially if you return to Aliz while it's in chaos."

She pushed a lock of hair that had blown into her face back over her shoulder. Her brows were pinched together, her eyes narrowed.

"I know that," she said finally. "I was angry with you—I'm still angry that you didn't consult me—but I know you did what I asked for when I accepted your help."

"Your safety is my priority, Veronica. No matter how angry I make you, or how much you might hate me for it."

She shook her head, looked away. "I don't hate you. Though it might be easier if I did." She drew in a long breath. "You kept me safe, and you did so when I was determined to put myself—and my people—in danger."

"I'd do it again, if the circumstances were the same."

"I know that, too." Her head dropped as she fixed her gaze on the sand at her feet. He wanted to pull her close and kiss the top of her head, but he did not do so. He stood with arms hanging at his sides.

He felt…useless in some ways. He'd brought her here, but he hadn't yet found who'd sent her the note or placed the doll on her bed. She was safe, but for how long? If her government was restored and she returned to Aliz, then what?

She wouldn't need him anymore. He would never see her again, except as a photograph in a newspaper.

She looked up, her eyes shining with unshed tears. "I wish I'd met you earlier, under different circumstances. Maybe neither of us would have any regrets then."

He couldn't stop himself from reaching out and lifting a strand of her hair. He loved the silken feel of it, the bright pale color. In the moonlight, it hung down her back like ropes of gossamer ribbon.

"Life is filled with regrets," he said.

He couldn't imagine not being able to touch her like this. He didn't want to imagine it.

She let out a deep sigh that slashed into his control. "Oh, Raj, if we don't learn from our mistakes, then what is the point?" He froze as she reached for him, her hand wrapping around the back of his neck while the other gripped his arm to steady herself as she stood on tiptoe.

He didn't resist as she pulled him down to her, didn't resist as her lips brushed his. He didn't close his eyes because he wanted to see her face while she kissed him. Her lashes dipped down, fanning long and silky beneath her eyes as her mouth skimmed across his.

The pressure was light, so light. Unbearable. He wanted to crush her to him, wanted to slide his tongue between her lips and feel her response.

"It's too late," she whispered against his mouth a moment later. "As you've pointed out more than once, you aren't the right man."

She took a step backward, breaking the contact, and then turned and started down the beach. He watched her as she found the path back up to the house, his heart a lead weight in his chest. He'd wanted her to realize the truth, hadn't he?

She had finally done so. And he wanted to howl.

Veronica found her way blindly up the side of the hill, then stumbled into her room and slapped the doors closed. Tears pricked her eyes. She was tired of fighting them, so she let them fall.

She'd lied. She'd stood there and lied to him when she'd told him he wasn't the right man. Because he was the man her heart wanted, though she tried to deny it. She'd realized it tonight, and she'd been running from the truth of it when she'd gone down to the beach.

How could she be so stupid? How could she have allowed herself to fall for him?

It was too soon.

He was too much.

He stunned her, quite simply. He was insightful, tender and tough. He made her feel safe. He'd even made her feel loved, though she knew he didn't love her.

But he was also wild, untamable. She'd known it, and yet she'd insisted on lying in the tiger's jaws. When he chewed her up and spit her out, she had no one to blame but herself. She stood in the middle of the room, tears falling as she dashed them angrily away, and wanted to scream. She'd been just fine until he'd come into her life! She'd been getting through the days, trying to heal, trying to live.

He'd ripped everything open again, made her feel, made her ache and want and need and love.

After a while, Veronica went into the bathroom and washed her face with cold water. Then she stripped off her gown and dropped it on the bed.

The bed was huge, a solid carved four-poster with white filmy netting hanging from it—and no way was she staying here tonight. No way was she sleeping in this giant bed, with Raj in the same house, knowing she couldn't go to him.

Knowing he would not come to her.

Veronica found a thin silk robe in her luggage and wrapped it around herself. Then she slipped into the hallway and toward the front doors. She would go down to the cottages, find Martine's quarters and sleep there tonight. If she were not under the same roof with Raj, she could breathe again. She could think and feel and not ache so much.

She found the front door and jerked it open—

Raj was standing on the other side, his hand poised over the handle. They stared at each other without speaking. He wasn't wearing a shirt, and her heart lodged in her throat. A pair of pajama bottoms sat low on his hips, the drawstring tied just loosely enough to allow his lean hip bones to protrude.

Not to mention the ridges of his abdominal muscles, so hard and tight beneath his broad chest. Her mouth went dry. Her brain refused to function. She tried to speak, but no sound came out.

"Going somewhere?" he asked, one eyebrow lifting sardonically.

"Yes," she managed to respond, her voice croaking out as if she'd been traveling across a desert with nothing to drink. She swallowed. "I was going to find Martine."

"Isn't it a bit late to dictate a letter?"

She couldn't admit to him that she'd wanted to escape this house. Wanted to escape him. It would give him too much power over her. As if he didn't have enough already. As if she weren't teetering on the edge of something that would change her forever.

"I thought of something important," she lied, lifting her chin.

"It's a distance to the cottages." His gaze slipped down her body. "And there are things you might not wish to meet in the dark. Especially dressed like that."

"I went to the beach in an evening gown," she pointed out.

"Not as far. Or as rich with vegetation."

She wanted to argue, but she took a step back, defeated. She wanted out, but she wasn't stupid. Who knew what manner of creatures waited on the path to the cottages? Bugs? Stinging bugs? Cobras?

Veronica shivered.

Raj came inside and closed the door. Locked it.

Her heart thundered in her ears. He was so close. Once more, so close. He smelled delicious, like the sea and wind and India.

"You're upset," he said softly.

"I'm not."

He lifted a finger, skimmed her cheek, tipped up her chin so he could look down into her eyes. The light in the entry came from the living area, warm and golden and spilling through the prism of glass that divided one area from another. Her breath stopped in her chest. Time seemed to stretch out between them, so fine and thin, like the thread spun out by the mythical Fates.

But would one of them cut it, or would it continue to spin?

"You make me want things I shouldn't," he said, his voice so husky and deep.

Her heart pounded in her temples, her throat, between her legs. "Who says you shouldn't? You? Are you not in control of your own destiny?"

His laugh was part groan. "You make it sound so simple, like one simply reaches a decision and starts down a new path."

"Don't they?"

"You know it's not true. You know that life throws things at you, and you do the best you can to deal with them. If you're lucky, you figure out what works for you, and you stick with it."

It was her turn to laugh. "And how is that working for you, Raj? Because I have no idea what I'm doing from one day to the next some-times. Maybe I should try your method."

His expression was troubled in the dim light. "You confuse things, Veronica."

A pinprick of pain pierced her, the hurt rip-pling outward as if someone had thrown a rock into a pond. "Don't patronize me. I'm not stu-pid, and I'm not confused."

"You confuse things for *me*," he said. "You make me question myself."

"Everyone should question his paradigm from time to time."

"Are you questioning yours?" he asked, taking a step closer to her. "Am I still the wrong man?"

His mouth was so close now, and her body was sizzling with heat and memory and need.

"You're completely wrong," she said. "I don't want you at all."

His smile was self-assured. Feral and sexy. "You're lying, Veronica."

He tilted his head, studying her. She endured his scrutiny, her heart thundering, her skin beg-ging for his touch.

Oh, God, she no longer cared. She just wanted him to touch her, to give her the bliss he'd given her two nights ago. She wanted to feel loved again, even if it wasn't quite true.

She thought she would go mad waiting.

"What do you plan to do about it?" she said, a heaviness settling in her abdomen, between her legs.

He smiled again, only this time it was filled with regret. "Nothing. The desire will have to be enough for both of us."

Furious tears stung the backs of her eyes. "Bravo, Raj. Once more, you're willing to sacrifice yourself on the altar of altruism for my sake. Whatever would I do without you to make decisions for me?"

His growl was not what she expected, but it sent a thrill through her belly nevertheless. "You can't have it both ways," he snapped. "You can't tell me I'm wrong for you and then look at me like I'm the only man who has what you need. So tell me what you want from me or get back to bed."

CHAPTER ELEVEN

TELL me what you want.

Such a simple statement, and so complicated all at once. So many things she wanted, and only one thing she would get from him. Only one thing he was willing to give.

Or perhaps he wasn't.

Perhaps he was simply trying to humiliate her. Perhaps the best thing she could do—for herself, for both of them—was to turn and go back to her bedroom.

Heart in her throat, she turned away and took two steps. And then, because she was frustrated and angry and hurt and confused, she turned back. Stood there staring at him while he stared back, no one saying anything, no one moving.

So many emotions and thoughts crashing through her—and one very big one that said, *Why are you doing this? Life is too short to play games. You know what life can do to you when you don't take it seriously.*

As soon as she thought the words, she understood something very fundamental about Raj. It was as if someone had pulled back a curtain and shown her an illuminated tablet upon which this particular truth was carved: he was accustomed to denying himself.

The little boy who'd never written that note to the Barbie-pink girl, who'd never gotten to go to her party or ask her to be his girlfriend, was standing here now, unwilling to take a chance. Because tomorrow might change everything. Because tomorrow he might move away again, and the party would happen without him. The girl would find another boyfriend. Nothing stayed the same in Raj's world, and he'd learned it was better not to get attached to anything just in case.

Her blood sang as if she'd just been shown a priceless secret. She understood what motivated him. She understood and she knew what she had to do.

Veronica untied the belt at her waist and let the robe slide down her shoulders to pool at her feet. She was only wearing the black lace thong she'd worn beneath the strapless gown, and nothing else. Her breasts pebbled as she stood there for what seemed an eternity, waiting for Raj to react.

"Veronica," he said. Choked, really.

"I know what *I* want," she said. "But I don't think you do. You think you have to deny yourself. But you don't, Raj. It's okay to want things. It's okay to want *me*. I don't expect anything out of you."

"You do," he said, his voice still strained. "You want the kind of life I can't give you."

She swallowed. "I don't think either one of us is ready for more at this point in our lives."

Though part of her ached for more, she didn't deserve it. She had to be real with herself. Because he would despise her if he knew what sort of person she really was. And she couldn't bear it if he did.

She closed the distance between them. They didn't touch. The heat emanating from his body touched her instead—enclosed her, enveloped her. He was on fire. It made her wonder how much she would sizzle when he actually made contact.

Then she slid her palms up his arms while his eyes glowed hot, over his biceps and hard pectoral muscles. His nipples were small, tight, and she tweaked them with her thumbs while he growled deep in his chest.

And then she told him what she wanted right

now. The words she used were graphically, shockingly raw.

She surprised herself. Surprised him if the way his eyes widened were any indication.

But then he was dropping to his knees in front of her, pressing his face to her bare belly, kissing a trail down her abdomen. Hooking his fingers into the material of her thong, he slipped it down her legs until she could step out of it.

Then he lifted one of her legs and put it over his shoulder while she gasped.

"Raj, not here!"

"Yes, here."

She gripped his shoulders to keep herself upright, but his mouth on her body, on her most sensitive spot, soon had her panting and gasping and thrusting her hips to increase the pressure. When she came a split second later, her knees buckled. Only his strong grip kept her standing.

And then he was on his feet, backing her against the wall. She wrapped her arms around his neck, kissed him, their tongues tangling urgently as he shifted her against him until her legs were wrapped around his waist and his hard shaft was at her entrance.

Veronica cried out as he plunged into her body. But it wasn't pain that caused her to do so. Somehow he knew, because he didn't hesitate to thrust again and again, harder, until she dragged her mouth from his and tilted her head back to moan her pleasure.

Oh, this was exactly what she wanted—what she needed. Raj, here like this. Raj, inside her, part of her. *Raj, Raj, Raj...*

"God, Veronica," he said, and she knew she'd been speaking aloud. She'd been telling him what she wanted, saying his name...

His mouth found her throat, his lips and tongue and teeth sending a shiver of delight racing down her spine, over her nerve endings, into her molten core. She was close, so close.

Raj made a sound of frustration. "Need more," he said, the words hot against her skin. "Need more of you."

And then he strode across the room, their bodies still joined, taking her somewhere, though she didn't know where until they were falling together and her back hit something soft.

He rose above her, his dark face so handsome and sexy as he worked to hold on to his control. She could see the restraint in his eyes, could see how he held a part of himself back, how he was still worried about hurting her in spite of his need.

"Give me all of you," she said. "I want all of you, Raj."

"Veronica—" Her name was a groan—so raw, so torn.

"I don't want you to hold back. If this is all we have, I don't want to miss anything."

They both knew it wasn't about the physical. That part was perfect. Amazing, hot and wonderful. His gaze was wild, his body throbbing inside hers, and yet she still wondered if she'd carried it too far, if he would withdraw and leave her lying here alone.

He was capable of it, she was certain, no matter the cost to his pleasure.

But then he groaned, his head dropping until his forehead touched hers, and she knew he'd surrendered. He kissed her, their mouths fusing so sweetly, so perfectly. He was still so hard inside her, but he didn't move. He simply kissed her, skimming the fingers of one hand over her face, as if he were learning her shape and texture by touch alone.

A tear leaked from her eye, slid down her temple. He kissed it away, kissed the tender skin of her cheek, the bones of her face. Love swelled inside her heart until she thought it would burst. She wanted to let it out, wanted to tell him how she felt, and yet it terrified her.

She was in love with him, and she couldn't tell him. So bittersweet, so shattering.

Veronica thrust her hands into his hair, curled them into his skin, slid them over his body. She wanted to know every part of him, the golden skin and eyes, the hard, sensual lips, the straight, regal nose. The hardness buried deep inside her.

"Oh, Raj," she gasped as he flexed his hips and sensation bolted through her, from her fingertips to her scalp, her toes to her nipples. Every part of her was alive and on fire for him.

"I love the way you say my name when I'm inside you," he growled. "So sexy, so needy."

"I am needy," she said, arching her back, trying to get him to move again. "I want more."

He withdrew from her, surged forward again. "More of this?"

"God, yes."

This time he obliged her, thrusting into her again and again, her body soaring as he drove her toward completion. There was nothing left between them. No barriers, no secrets, no lies— nothing but raw, hungry emotion. Their bodies rose and fell together, giving and taking, taking and giving.

She wanted to feel like this forever, and yet it had to end. Finally, she could hold back no longer. The pounding pressure started a ripple of sensation deep inside that engulfed her senses.

The only word she could say, the only one that would form on her tongue, was his name.

And then he was tumbling over the edge right behind her, grasping her buttocks and lifting her to him as he came. Her name on his lips sounded so raw it gave her a thrill. His breath in her ear was rapid, as if he'd been running.

Veronica closed her eyes, her heart racing in time with his, blood pounding and body singing. She was happy. Right this moment, she was so incredibly happy. She felt as if she was flying and she didn't want to look down, didn't want to see the scorpion waiting to strike. She didn't want this to end.

But it would. She knew it would.

"You've killed me," he said. "Sacrificed me for your selfish pleasure. I'm done in."

Veronica laughed, ran her fingers up the damp skin of his back. "Oh, yes, my evil plan is complete. I intend to drain you, Rajesh Vala. Leave you an empty husk, unable to ever get it up again for any other woman."

She said it jokingly, and yet the thought of Raj with another woman pierced her to the bone.

"Don't do that," he said softly, skimming his lips along her jaw, the shell of her ear. "Don't put something between us that doesn't exist."

She shuddered beneath him, her heart pinching tight in her chest. "I'm simply being realistic," she said. Because there would be other women in his life, once she was gone. He was too sensual, too male. He couldn't be tamed—but he could be caught, for a short time anyway.

He tweaked her nipple, made a sound of approval when she gasped. "This is what's real, Veronica."

A short while later, he carried her to his bed and proved that he was perfectly capable of sacrificing himself for her pleasure yet again.

Raj came awake as the sea breeze blew into the windows and rustled the filmy netting. The covers had been flung off long ago. Beside him, Veronica was curled into a ball with her back to him. He traced a fingertip along her shoulder, her hip. Already, his body was stirring, wanting her again.

She was a fire in his blood, this woman. She had been since the first moment he'd seen her. He spared half a thought for Brady, but she'd never been Brady's to begin with. Veronica had chosen *him,* and he would not feel guilty for it.

He kissed her shoulder, cupped a breast in his palm. She came awake with a smile, turning sleepily in his arms.

She was as hot for him as he was for her.

Thank God. Pushing him onto his back, she straddled him and sank down onto him with a groan. He closed his eyes, his body pulsing inside hers. He could live this way. He could wake every morning like this, Veronica undulating her hips and making him crazy with need.

He gripped her thighs, slowing her movements before it was over too fast. When he looked up at her, her pale hair was swinging around her breasts as if she were Lady Godiva riding through the town square. Her nipples were hard little points that he wanted to suck.

Except that he couldn't move. If he moved, it would be over too quickly.

She arched her back, lifted her arms and pulled her hair off her body. "Oh, yes," she said, her voice little more than a throaty whisper. "Like that. Just there."

He suddenly wanted to shatter her control, wanted to prove he could, wanted her wild and wriggling beneath him. He wanted to know that she was his, that he was the one who made her quiver and sigh and cry out with pleasure.

With a quick movement, he flipped her over, driving deeper into her body. Her legs wrapped around his hips, her teeth biting into her lush lower lip as she arched toward him.

He lost whatever thread of control he'd been

holding on to, driving into her until she shattered beneath him with a sharp, hard cry. But he didn't stop there. He couldn't. He kept stroking into her until she caught on fire again, until his body was burning up with hers, until they both plunged over the edge and crashed onto the rocks below.

Mine, he thought. *Mine.*

It was sometime later when he woke a second time. Veronica was asleep again, her lush body pale in the morning light. Her skin was red in places, and he realized he needed to shave. He climbed from the bed with a yawn and a languid stretch before making his way to the bathroom and turning on the shower.

If he had any strength at all, he'd make love to Veronica in the shower. He imagined holding her against the slippery wall, imagined driving up into her body, and was half tempted to go wake her when he began to harden.

Instead, he got dressed and headed for the dining room. Breakfast would be waiting, as well as his morning reports. He took a seat at the table and tore into the fragrant *dosa*.

It had taken him several visits to convince the housekeeper that he didn't want a traditional English breakfast every morning when he was in residence. Now that he'd been coming to Goa for the past few years, they'd slipped into enough of a routine that he could expect masala *dosa* in the mornings unless he specifically asked for full English.

He flipped through the reports, finding nothing he didn't already know in any of them. The doors to the terrace were open, and air fragrant with the spices being used in the kitchen blew gently through the house.

"Good morning."

Raj looked up from the report he'd been reading. Veronica waltzed into the room, her hair a gorgeous mess pinned on top of her head, her lips full and swollen from his kisses, her skin glowing. She'd slipped into one of his shirts, which she'd rolled at the cuffs, the tails hitting her about midthigh.

He'd always thought it a not-so-subtle attempt at claiming ownership when a woman put on one of his shirts the morning after sex. As if she were saying he belonged to her now that they'd spent the night in bed.

But with Veronica, all he could think was that she belonged to him and that his shirt was a lucky bastard.

"Don't gape, Raj," she said, grabbing a piece of *dosa* and a cup of chai that seemed to magically appear when she did, before she turned and went to stand in the open door. Beyond, the sea sparkled in the sun.

Raj went to stand behind her, breathing in the scent of her hair. Aching to touch her again, right now. Right here.

"It's so lovely. I don't think I've ever felt more relaxed." She turned and winked up at him. "But I don't think the relaxed part has anything to do with the view."

"It's a very nice view," he said—though he didn't mean the scenery.

She laughed and pulled the V of his shirt closed where it had gaped over her breasts. "Such a man."

"Definitely."

She took a sip of the chai and sighed. "It's odd to think it's nearly Christmas, isn't it, when it's so warm?"

"I like it warm."

She turned to him. "You don't like a traditional Christmas, with snow and hot chocolate and a big evergreen tree?"

He shrugged. "Actually, I don't care for Christmas much. It's too commercial."

She blinked. "But what about presents? Surely you like presents."

"It doesn't have to be Christmas for presents."

"No, that's true. I just remember such fabulous

Christmases when I was a little girl. When my mother was still alive, my father would take us to Switzerland or Bavaria. He'd rent a chalet, and we'd ski and do all the traditional things. It was wonderful. I never feel like it's Christmas unless I'm cold." She grabbed a slice of mango from the table. "What's your favorite Christmas memory?"

A dart of pain pierced him. He started to make something up, to give an answer that would satisfy her and let her keep chattering happily away.

But he couldn't seem to do it. The urge to speak the truth built in his gut until he was nearly bursting with it.

"I don't have any. My mother couldn't afford Christmas."

She'd done her best when he was small, finding some cast-off toy at the thrift shop or signing him up for whatever local program gave to needy children. But the older he'd gotten—the further she'd sunk into her addiction and depression—she'd given up even trying.

Veronica's sky-blue eyes grew cloudy. She reached out, squeezed his arm. "I'm sorry."

"It's fine. I'm not a kid anymore. It doesn't matter."

"But you must have been sad when you were little. I'm sorry for that."

He slipped a hand into the small of her back,

pulled her in tight. His body wasted little time
in reacting to the soft, warm feel of her pressed
against him.

She tilted her head back to look up at him.
He traced a finger along the beautiful line of
her mouth. "It was a long time ago. And I can
think of a few things you can give me if you
really want to give me presents."

She ran her free hand up his arm, threaded her
fingers into the hair at his nape. She looked troubled still—but then she smiled a wicked smile
and he forgot everything but her.

"Oh, I imagine I could think of a few of my
own."

Veronica couldn't remember ever being as happy
as she was with Raj. It was her second day in
Goa, and he'd taken her into one of the small
villages along the coast. They were currently
strolling through a market, hand in hand. She
knew they had security.

Except the men Raj employed weren't dressed
in suits and sporting headsets. They blended in,
unlike her own staff had done in London.

She enjoyed it because it made her feel carefree. It was an illusion, but she was determined
to take pleasure in it anyway.

"We can't stay long," Raj said as they

meandered between stalls filled with fresh fruits and vegetables—tomatoes, cucumbers, onions, squashes, coconut, mangoes, nubby jackfruit—and dried spices and chilies that were so colorful she wanted to stop and stare at them so she could remember just how vibrant colors like orange and red and brown could truly be.

The women wore colorful saris, the men *kurtas* and sandals. There were goats, cows, the occasional painted elephant and a few Western tourists in their T-shirts and backpacks. The market was jammed with sound and movement, and she loved it.

"Thank you for bringing me," she said. "It's marvelous."

He smiled down at her, tweaked the sunglasses on her nose. "It's a risk, but I think no one will recognize you. You look very mysterious."

"And you stand out like a peacock," she grumbled as a woman turned her head to look back at Raj as she walked past them. The woman smiled. Veronica felt a stab of jealousy when Raj smiled back.

"The better to draw attention away from you," he said, leading her down another alleyway in the market.

Eventually, he stopped in a shadowed alcove

and pulled her into his arms. She'd chosen to wear linen trousers and a big cotton shirt today. She'd belted the white shirt at her waist with a broad belt, and put on a straw hat that she'd found on a shelf in her bedroom. She'd been wearing ballet flats, but Raj had bought her a pair of beaded sandals as soon as they'd arrived in town.

Now, she braced her hands on his chest and gazed up at him through dark sunglasses. He was looking at her like as if was his favorite snack.

The thought made her shiver.

"I'm glad you're enjoying yourself today," he said. And then he bent and kissed her, as if he couldn't get enough of her. She felt the same, her arms going around his neck, her body arching into his. The alcove he'd pulled her into was private, but not that private.

He broke the kiss, though not before she felt the effect of it on his body.

"I can think of something else I'd enjoy even more," she purred.

"Me, too," he said. "But man cannot live on sex alone. We have to eat."

Veronica smiled. "I love to eat."

"Good, because I'm taking you somewhere special."

He led her from the market and down a wide street lined with wooden buildings painted in bright colors. People turned their heads as Raj and Veronica walked past, though she knew it was because they were looking at him and not her. Then Raj led her into a nondescript red building whose wooden facade had seen better days.

It was sun-bleached and dusty, with palms overhanging the entry. Inside, the building was clean, but Raj led her through the room and out the back to a plank deck overlooking the bright blue sea. Several tables were scattered on the deck, topped with grass umbrellas, and Raj took her to the farthest one and pulled out a rickety wooden chair for her.

The proprietor came bustling over, his chatter a mixture of English and Konkani. He seemed to know Raj, and they spent a few minutes conversing in both languages before the man clapped Raj on the shoulder and said the food would be out soon. Then he disappeared into the kitchen and started shouting orders.

"You're wondering why this place is special," Raj said.

Veronica shrugged a shoulder. The clank of metal and cacophony of voices in the kitchen had somehow blended together until it became white noise. "It seems like the kind of place that wouldn't get a second look from most tourists," she admitted.

"Exactly. That's part of it, since it's not over-run by tourists. The other part is that I was eating at this very table one afternoon when I decided to buy a house here."

She reached for his hand, knowing that he was sharing something important with her. Raj, who wasn't vulnerable or weak in the least, had experienced something profound and been moved into action by it. Her heart throbbed with love for him.

He squeezed her fingers. "It may not seem like a momentous step, but it was for me. This house here was the first I ever bought for myself. Until then, I'd lived in rented condos or hotel rooms." He turned to gaze out at the turquoise water. "Actually, it was the first real home I ever had."

Something in his voice carved out a hollow space inside her that ached for him. He was a little boy who'd never had Christmas, a man who'd waited—though he'd had money—to buy a home for himself.

"You never lived very long in one place, did you?" When he'd told her they'd moved a lot, she'd assumed he meant every few months or so.

When you were a kid, any upheaval was traumatic. Now, she was beginning to think it had been something more.

He turned back to her, his golden gaze both hard and sad at once. "The one thing I wanted more than anything as a child was to be able to have a room of my own. My own bed, my own walls, my own toys. If I unpacked my suitcase—when I still had a suitcase—we moved again. So I stopped unpacking. Then one day it was gone and everything we owned could fill the backseat of the rusty car my mom somehow managed to keep."

"Raj," she said, her eyes filling with tears. She wanted to hold him, wanted to tell him she was sorry. She wanted to take his pain away.

He leaned forward and kissed her, swiftly and surely. "Don't feel sorry for me, Veronica. I didn't tell you so you would feel sorry for me."

She spread her palm over his jaw, caressed him. "I don't. I'm just grateful you felt you could tell me."

He turned and kissed her palm. "There's no one else I'd rather share it with."

The words were simple, but they choked her up. She dropped her gaze, stared at the bright tablecloth. If he knew the truth about her, he wouldn't think so highly of her, would he?

She had to tell him. "Raj…"

"Yes?"

But a waiter walked out with fresh *papadum* and sauces and she lost her nerve.

"Nothing," she said.

The rest of the meal came soon after. They talked and ate and enjoyed the view before Raj paid the bill and they walked back out to the street.

Soon, they were on their way to his house, the cars rolling through a beautiful tropical landscape. Goa was such a land of contrasts, she realized, as they passed a temple with a tall, conical bell tower, it's layers crowned with carvings and dotted with arched windows. A short distance away they passed a distinctly Portuguese church, its grounds scattered with tourists wielding cameras.

It was a beautiful place, and she could see why Raj loved it so much.

Though she'd intended to meet with her staff again this afternoon, all it took was one hot look from the man she loved to make her amend her plans. They spent the next couple of hours in bed, wrapped in each other, living off of kisses, whispered words and slow, deep thrusts that took them to heaven and back. It would be so easy to forget the world when nothing seemed more important than what took place when they were alone together.

But later, when the sun was sinking into the sea and they were dozing in each other's arms, there was a knock on the door.

"Yes," Raj managed to say, his voice husky with sleep.

"There is a call for the president," someone said.

Veronica looked up, met his gaze. She didn't want the outside world intruding, not yet. But she had no choice. They both knew it.

"Who is it?" Raj asked.

"Someone named Monsieur Brun."

CHAPTER TWELVE

VERONICA took the call on the terrace after hurriedly dragging on her clothes and wrapping an elastic band around her tangle of hair. Her chief of staff was in attendance, as well as her secretary.

Raj watched them all as Veronica sat like a queen—*a rumpled queen,* he thought with a surge of possessiveness—and spoke to the former president in French. Raj didn't understand French, but he could tell that Veronica was cool and professional.

The sun was a bright orange ball now, the sea beneath it purple and black. High above the setting sun, bright stars were winking into existence like sequins against the midnight-blue background of the night sky.

But Raj was focused on Veronica, and on the two people watching her so intently.

Martine glanced up at him, then quickly looked away. Her fingers hooked together in front of her body, her knuckles whitening. She was afraid.

But Veronica's eyes widened and Raj's attention snapped to her. Her chief of staff thrust a fist into the air in triumph as Veronica said something to the man on the phone, her voice laced with shock.

Martine seemed pale, her big brown eyes blinking in surprise. And then Veronica was speaking rapidly, smiling openly and nodding. Another few moments and she put the phone down again. Then she jumped up and hugged Georges and Martine before throwing herself into his arms.

"Brun has denounced the police chief," she said. "He is about to hold a press conference and publicly come out in support of me." Her eyes were shiny with tears. "He loves Aliz and wants the best for her, just like I do. Oh, Raj, this means I can continue working for my people. This is truly the best day ever."

He should be happy, and yet he felt as if she'd thrust a hot knife into his chest and twisted it. He'd begun to enjoy having her here, having her to himself. But when she returned to her life as president, he would return to his life, as well.

And it wasn't a life that included her.

"That's wonderful," he said, because he had to say something.

She squeezed him, pressing her cheek to his chest. "We can go to Aliz now," she told him. "It's not quite like here, but I think you'll like it. I want to show you everything, and I want you to have Christmas with me. It'll be wonderful."

He was numb. Absolutely numb. "Of course," he replied. Because now was not the time to say anything different. Now was not the time to hang a dark cloud over her happiness. There would be time later to talk, time to explain. Time to return to reality.

She hugged him again, then turned and started talking with her people. He watched her, watched the gestures of her long, slim fingers, the slide of her throat as she spoke, the way she talked so fast and excitedly that Martine could barely take the dictation.

For her sake, he tried to imagine it. Tried to imagine himself in Aliz, with her. She would live in the presidential palace, of course. He would visit her there whenever he had the time. It could work.

But it couldn't work. She deserved better. She deserved a man who could love her and give her the family she wanted. Without hesitation or reservation. He loved being with her, and he

could happily spend the next several months—
years, maybe—in her bed without ever wanting to leave.

But it wasn't fair to her. He knew what she
wanted out of life because she'd told him.

He did not want the same thing, and it wasn't
fair to let her believe he did. He'd known it
wasn't going to last. He just hadn't thought it
was going to end so soon.

It was late when Veronica wrapped up her meetings with her staff. There were more phone
calls to be made, plans to discuss and Monsieur
Brun's speech on CNN to watch. The chief of
police hadn't surrendered yet, but he would
soon. He had no support, and his last lifeline—
the hope that Brun would be reinstated—was
gone.

Veronica had done a set of interviews by
phone, speaking with several news reporters
live on various television and radio programs,
and now she was exhausted. The situation in
Aliz had exploded onto the international scene
in greater force with Brun's speech.

Everyone wanted to know where she was,
but she'd kept that information private. She
just couldn't bear to have the press show up at

Raj's door after everything they'd shared here together.

She found Raj on the terrace, a laptop computer open and glowing as he studied the information there. He looked up when she arrived, his eyes flickering over her before settling on her face again.

The hunger she usually saw in his gaze was missing. Her stomach did a somersault. Resolutely, she walked over to his side and touched him, stroked her fingers along his jaw. He caught her hand in his, then removed it from his skin with a quick kiss to her palm. He stood and moved away before she could reach for him again.

She stood there, stinging with the ache of rejection, hoping she was reading the situation wrong.

Knowing she was not.

"So this is how it ends," she said, her throat aching.

He looked up, as if he was surprised she'd said it instead of pretending. And then he pushed his fingers through his hair. "I think it's best, don't you?"

"Why is it best? What rulebook says there is a specific way we have to do this? We—" she swallowed, knowing she couldn't say the word she really wanted to say, especially since she only knew it was true on her part "—enjoy each other."

"We hardly know each other, Veronica." He looked away, his jaw firming. "We've had sex, nothing more."

Sex, nothing more.

Oh, God.

"*I* thought there was more."

He swore. "This is why I tried not to be so weak, why I tried to deny myself when I wanted you. Because it won't work, Veronica. We both know it."

She clenched her fists at her sides, her eyes blurring. Angrily, she dashed the tears away. She was not about to cry. Not now, not when she'd just gotten a second chance in Aliz. She should feel happy, triumphant—instead, she felt desolate, ruined, as if nothing mattered.

It was too similar to the way she'd felt a few months ago. And that angered her far more than anything else ever could.

"I didn't realize you were a coward, Raj."

His eyes flashed as he glared at her. "I know what you're trying to do. It won't work." He closed the distance between them, gripped her shoulders in his strong hands. "Didn't you listen to a damn thing I told you earlier? I don't know *how* to have a home, a family. I don't want those things. You do, and I won't give you false hope just because I'm addicted to you."

A part of her—a tiny part—soared when he said he was addicted to her. But it wasn't enough, she knew that. Wasn't enough for him or for her. It hurt to think that it was only sex between them. But for him, it was.

"You won't even try," she said.

"No," he replied, letting her go again. "I won't. Because I know who I am, Veronica. I've had a lot of years to learn. And I won't hurt you by trying to be something I'm not."

She wrapped her arms around her body, trying to stave off the sudden chill that threatened to make her teeth chatter. It wasn't cold in the least, but she felt as if he'd turned into a block of ice—and she was freezing simply from being too close. "God forbid you challenge your own assumptions."

"Veronica—"

"No," she snapped, taking a step closer to him again, jabbing her finger into his chest. "If you're so damn smart, and know so much, then why didn't you just tell me no in the first place? No matter how much I wanted you, you could have said no. You could have spared us both."

He raised his hands as if to surrender. "You're

right. I could have. I didn't because I'm human. Because I can be a selfish bastard. Because I still want the things I know I can't have."

"After everything I told you," she said, sucking in a harsh breath. She couldn't complete the sentence without screaming.

"Yes, after everything. Because I'm a man, and you're a damn sexy woman who was hot for me. It'd take a saint to say no to you."

Fury swelled inside her until she thought she would burst if she didn't act. She wanted to slap him, wanted to smack the arrogance right off his face. But she couldn't hit him, couldn't hit anyone.

It was so, so wrong.

And it was her fault, too. She wasn't blameless in this. It was her fault that she'd told herself whatever he could give her was enough.

It wasn't.

"I trusted you, Raj. Losing my baby was the most devastating thing that ever happened to me. I didn't think I could feel again, didn't think I—"

She pressed a fist to her chest, throat aching. She couldn't say another word. If she did, she would scream. He was looking at her, his expression stark.

Well, that's how she felt, too. Stark. Empty.

"You don't need me, Veronica," he said. "You're strong enough and brave enough on your own. And you'll find what you're looking for. Someday."

"I'm not so sure," she said, half to herself. "I knew this was inevitable." She tossed her hair defiantly. "Hell, maybe you *are* right. Maybe it's better this way. Because you wouldn't have wanted me once you knew the truth."

His gaze sharpened, his body stilling. As if he were a hunter scenting prey.

"The truth?" He sounded so dangerous.

She didn't care. What did it matter? She looked him in the eye. "It's my fault my baby died. So you see, even if you wanted a family, I'm not the sort of woman you'd want to take that chance with."

He swore, a rude word she'd never heard him use before. "I've spent enough time with you to know that's not true. You aren't responsible for your miscarriage, no matter what kind of crazy idea you've got into your head about it."

Anguish ate her from the inside out. "Don't tell me I'm not responsible! You weren't there. I didn't know I was pregnant, Raj. I kept drinking, kept staying out late and having a good time— by the time I knew I was pregnant, the damage had been done."

He put his hands on her shoulders—firmly—and forced her to look at him. "Women don't lose babies because they drink alcohol, Veronica. Haven't you ever seen a drug addict have a child? The baby is usually born with devastating health problems, but the baby is *born*. A few drinks didn't kill your child."

Her stomach was a solid ball of pain. "You don't know that."

His jaw clenched, his eyes glittering with some emotion she couldn't identify. "I do know. I've seen it. My mother was a drug addict. Not when I was young, but as I grew older. And I saw the kind of people she did drugs with. Believe me, if they didn't lose the children they were carrying because of what they did, you definitely didn't."

She sucked in a breath, refused to let it become a sob. She wanted to believe him. She'd always wanted to believe, but she'd never been able to. The doctors had told her it wasn't her fault, that the miscarriage would have happened regardless. She'd just never believed them.

Raj pulled her into his embrace, held her tight for a long time. She closed her eyes, breathed in his scent, her heart hurting so much she wanted to fall asleep and not wake up for a hundred years.

Because she knew, before he said it, that he was still saying goodbye.

"You deserve happiness, Veronica. That's why I'm letting you go."

Early the next morning, they left for the ten-hour flight to Aliz. Raj purposely kept himself away from Veronica for the duration. She never once looked at him, so he had plenty of opportunity to watch her. She was pale. Her hair was pulled back into a loose knot on her head, and she wore a black dress with a jacket and heels. There were circles under her eyes, and the tip of her nose was red, as if she'd been crying recently.

It gutted him to think she had.

Still, she was beautiful. Remote and regal, more like the Veronica he'd met the first night in London. The one who would never deign to lower herself to sleep with a bastard like him. Better for them both if she hadn't.

He'd lain awake last night, his body aching for her. His heart aching for her. That was a new sensation, but he'd shoved it down deep and slapped a lid on it. He had no room for sentimentality, not with her, not with anyone. If he let himself care, even the tiniest bit, tomorrow something would happen and it'd be time to move on again. He couldn't unpack the suitcase, no matter how much he wanted to do so.

Except that he did care, damn it. When she'd stood there, her eyes shining with pain, and told him she was to blame for what had happened to her, he'd thought he would have to punch something. Preferably Andre Girard.

She'd been living with so much pain and guilt. She'd needed someone to stand beside her during that time, and there'd been no one.

A little voice told him he could stand with her now, but he shoved it away. He'd made the decision that was best for them both, and he couldn't go back on it simply because his heart felt as if it were being ground to powder.

Now, he was taking her back to Aliz and leaving one of his best teams there to protect her. They would also train the presidential guard on proper procedures before they left Aliz permanently.

He never wanted to worry about her safety again. He'd gotten the reports on the people she'd had with her in London; nothing stood out. No one had any reason to want to harm her, which brought him back to square one. The security guard who'd been dismissed had to have been in the employ of someone in Aliz.

It wasn't the former president, but it could

have certainly been the police chief. He could have found out about the baby and decided to use that to frighten her. Perhaps he'd reasoned that if Veronica didn't want to return to Aliz, his power grab stood a better chance of being successful.

When they landed in Aliz, the television cameras were waiting. The tarmac was packed with supporters bearing signs with Veronica's name, with slogans, with the name of her hit song. They chanted and laughed and sang as she exited the plane and descended the stairs like a queen.

Veronica was so poised as she waved and smiled. His heart flipped. He was so proud of her, though he had no right to be. She wasn't his.

She stepped up to the microphone then and delivered a stirring speech about freedom and democracy and the rule of law. Monsieur Brun had wisely stayed away in order to prove that he really did want the torch to pass to his successor. The media pelted her with questions, all of which she answered expertly. She took a last question, and then thanked them all before turning away.

"Is it true that you and the CEO of Vala Security International are dating, Madam President?" a tabloid reporter shouted.

He watched Veronica's shoulders stiffen, watched her turn back to the microphone. Her cheeks were full of color, but she looked so lovely that no one would think it was anything other than her natural beauty shining through.

"That was a cover," she said. "So Mr. Vala and his team could get close to me without alerting those who might wish me harm."

"But you've just spent three days in Goa, at his home. Why there?"

Veronica's smile didn't waver. "Because we believed I might be in danger. It was prudent not to broadcast my whereabouts to the world at large."

"Did you sleep with him?"

A collective gasp went up from the crowd, and then a buzz of anger began in the ranks of the loyal people who'd come out to welcome home their president.

Veronica laughed that bright, tinkling laugh of hers. For some reason, it pierced him to the bone.

And then she turned and pointed at him. "Look at that man," she said. "Is he not gorgeous? Tall and exotic, beautiful like a tiger." She paused for a long moment, her eyes locked on him—angry, accusatory, hurt—before she turned back to the microphone. "But I assure you, there is nothing between us. Mr. Vala is all business. He does not know the meaning of fun."

A ripple of laughter went through the crowd as she waved and turned away. He had to give it to her—she knew how to work the media. He had no doubt that everything she'd ever done had been carefully orchestrated for the fullest effect. Veronica was no idiot. She'd effectively marginalized him with that brief show.

It had been a brilliant maneuver.

They made their way to the waiting limos and on to the presidential palace—which was actually quite small by palatial standards, though definitely ornate.

Raj spent the morning with his team and Veronica's security staff, going over plans and procedures for her safety during appearances and travel.

Afterward, he found her at an antique French desk in a spacious and bright office. Beyond the windows, the Mediterranean sparkled in the sunshine. Not as wild and untamable as Goa, but pretty nevertheless.

She looked up, her pen poised over a document, Georges hovering with his hand on the paper, ready to take it away as soon as she finished. She scrawled her signature and smiled at the man. He took the paper, glancing up at Raj with a disapproving look as he passed.

Veronica sat back and folded her arms over her chest. He tried not to think of her breasts, of how perfect they were. How her dusky nipples had grown so tight and sensitive when he'd gazed on her naked body.

How they tasted in his mouth, how every glorious inch of her felt beneath his hands.

Goddamn it.

"I'm leaving," he said tightly. "My people will stay as long as you need them, and I'll only be a phone call away if necessary."

"Thank you for…" She cleared her throat and looked away. The sunlight was behind her, limning her pale golden hair like a halo. He'd never felt so rotten in his life. "Thank you for making sure I was safe."

"My pleasure." As soon as he said it, he knew they were the wrong words.

Her eyes narrowed. "And thank you for the sex," she said. "I don't know how I'd have survived without you to scratch my itch."

"Veronica, you don't have to do this."

"Do what?" she asked. "Make you feel like a bastard? I really think I do. It makes me feel better, for a short time anyway. If it's any comfort, I'll feel like hell ten minutes after you've walked out the door."

"It isn't a comfort," he said. "I never wanted to hurt you."

She shrugged. "Maybe I'm not hurt. Maybe I'm just a bit angry that I'm not the one calling it off."

"You'll thank me later," he said.

"I seem to remember you said that to me once before. And I told you then that I would decide what was best for me. That hasn't changed."

"You're truly an amazing woman, Veronica."

"Not amazing enough."

"Don't play the wounded martyr," he snapped.

Her eyes flashed. "Look who's talking about being a martyr. The man who would sacrifice even the prospect of happiness for a stale idea about himself that he refuses to let go."

Her words had the power to slice deep.

But she was a hypocrite, and he wouldn't let her get away with it. Not because he was angry, but because he wanted her to finally allow herself to heal.

"Have you decided to stop blaming yourself for your miscarriage?"

Her head dropped, her throat sliding as she swallowed heavily. "You're right about that," she said softly. "And unless I'm willing to let go of my guilt, I can hardly ask you to do the same, can I?"

She looked up again, speared him with that determined look he'd grown to love.

"I've been thinking hard since yesterday, Raj. And I'm done with guilt. As much as I can be. I don't think I'll ever completely forgive myself, but I'm going to learn to accept that things happen for a reason."

"I'm glad to hear it."

Her phone buzzed. They looked at each other over the blinking light for several moments. She seemed to be waiting for him to say something.

"Goodbye, Veronica."

Veronica finished the call with the Moroccan ambassador and hung up the phone. Raj was gone, no doubt on his way back to the airport and then on to wherever he had decided to call home for the moment. She wanted to scream. He'd left her, and she felt so bare and raw inside.

The room was quiet. Empty. She could hear the noise outside the window, of gulls and boats, of tradesmen yelling to each other across the way, of cars and horns and everyday noise.

But she was still empty. Desolate.

He'd gone away. The man she loved had been

unable to love her back. It hurt so much she thought she might die of it.

She wouldn't, of course.

She thought of the lonely man who'd told her about living in a car, about being afraid to unpack a suitcase, about buying his first home, and her heart ached for everything that he'd suffered. They were a damaged pair, the two of them.

Veronica shoved back from her desk and strode through the office. Martine slapped the phone down, as if she felt guilty being caught talking, but Veronica could care less. In fact, she was getting tired of Martine's hangdog looks. The last thing she needed was someone who made her feel even worse.

"I'm going to my apartment," she said. "I need to change."

Martine nodded and Veronica swept out of the office and down the hallway toward the private wing that held the president's apartment. Madame Brun had decorated the private rooms of the old French Baroque palace in her own taste, and Veronica hated it. It was Marie Antoinette all the way, with fluffy ruffled things, mirrors and delicate furniture upon which one was afraid to sit for fear of collapsing the spindly legs.

One of these days, she would redecorate. But

right now, it was hardly important compared to everything else that was required of her.

Damn it, she *would* do a good job. For Aliz, for everyone who'd believed in her. Just as soon as she had some time alone, as soon as she collected herself and felt more normal, she was calling Signor Zarella. It was time to press him for a commitment, and she wasn't taking no for an answer. She had to accomplish something positive or she would go mad.

She went into her bedroom and stripped out of her clothes. A shower and a fresh outfit would do her good. When she finished, she stepped from the shower and dried herself vigorously. Then she wrapped the towel around her body and went back into her bedroom to find a different outfit.

She came up short, her heart rocketing as she realized she wasn't alone. But then she saw who it was. She put a hand over her chest, felt the pounding of her heart. "Martine. You scared me."

"I'm sorry, Miss St. Germaine." Tears flowed down Martine's cheeks.

"What's the matter, Martine?" Veronica said, taking a step toward her secretary.

Veronica stopped when Martine shook her head. "I'm sorry," she said again, her hand lifting, her arm stiff and straight.

It took Veronica only a split second to realize what was wrong.

Martine had a gun.

CHAPTER THIRTEEN

Raj had just climbed into the car that would take him back to the airport when his phone buzzed. Dread settled in his stomach like a lead ball as he listened to the man on the other end.

Then he was yelling at the driver to stop and shoving open the car door at the same time.

If something happened to Veronica, he would never forgive himself.

His staff was already making their way to her office, he knew, but he broke into a run anyway. When he reached the ornate office, it was empty. Worse, the outer office where her secretary sat was also empty.

He made a hard dash to her private residence. Two of his men were already there, knocking on the door.

Raj pushed past them and into the interior of Veronica's apartment. The gaudy living area was quiet. Just then, a muffled thump and a cry came from the direction of the bedroom. Raj sprinted, drawing the concealed weapon he carried, and kicked open the double doors.

Veronica was naked in the center of the room, a gun hanging limply from her hand. She swayed on her feet, her eyes wide. Another woman lay on the floor, curled in a ball, sobbing. Veronica looked up at him with glassy eyes.

He went and wrapped his arms tightly around her. She was trembling. He took the gun from her fingers and unloaded it with one hand before tossing it onto the bed. Belatedly, he remembered her state of undress. He retrieved the towel lying on the floor, draped it around her. It was damp and cool, but it was all he had.

His men came to lift up Martine and take her away.

"Don't hurt her," Veronica said as Martine screamed.

"They won't, I promise you."

The room was quiet once Martine and the bodyguards were gone. Veronica lifted her head. Her eyes were red-rimmed. It tore him apart. She reached out as if to touch his face, let her hand drop when she thought better of it.

Despair tore into his gut. He'd done that to her. He'd made her wary of him, and he hated it.

"I'm sorry, Veronica," he said.

She sucked in a shaky breath. Clung to him.

As much as he knew he should set her away, should put distance between them, he couldn't do it. He loved the feel of her in his arms. He wanted to hold her for as long as he could.

His arms tightened around her. He'd almost lost her.

"Martine's mother…" she said.

"I know. I just found out."

"Madame Brun was behind it all," she said. "She probably talked the police chief into doing what he did."

"Some people don't deal well with the loss of power." In this case, it was the wife rather than the husband, who, though disappointed in the outcome of the election, was a true politician.

"She threatened to take away Martine's mother's pension if Martine didn't do what she wanted. Martine spied on me, Raj. She told Madame Brun about the baby, and she pasted together the letter and put the doll in my bed."

"I know. I just got the report. Her mother worked for the Bruns for many years, and lives in an old-age home paid for by the pension she earned from them. If it were taken away, she'd be homeless. Or worse, with the economic situation in Aliz."

Veronica looked fierce for a moment. "I wouldn't have allowed that to happen if she'd only come to me! I'd have taken her mother in, paid the pension, whatever it took. Martine was my secretary for two years! I thought she knew me better than that."

"I imagine she was just scared. And I doubt she ever believed Madame Brun would ask her to…" He looked at the gun lying on the bed, so dark and deadly and gleaming blue in the light. He couldn't speak the words he was thinking. *To kill you.* "How did you get the gun?"

"All I had was the towel," Veronica said. "I reacted without thinking. I threw it at her."

Ice formed in his veins. She'd thrown a towel at an armed woman.

"You were lucky."

She nodded, her arms tightening around his waist. "I couldn't let it end like this. Not after everything."

My God, she was brave. And incredible. In another life, he'd have probably hired her to work for him. With training, she'd have made a hell of a security professional. Except that he couldn't bear the thought of her in danger.

Raj tipped her head back so he could see into her eyes. She was frightened, but not to the point of shock. Not yet anyway.

Her gaze dropped to his mouth. And, damn, but he couldn't stop himself from kissing her.

Softly, sweetly. He needed to know she was real, that she was still here and still capable of responding. That he wasn't imagining it. That he hadn't actually walked in on something much worse and started to hallucinate that she was unharmed.

Her mouth opened, her tongue tangling with his as she moaned softly. And then she was arching her body into his and he was pulling her closer, pressing her against the evidence of his need for her.

She broke the kiss first, her body stiffening in his embrace. He could tell the moment everything changed, and he let her go. His heart, his body, cried out in protest, but he loosened his grip and she stepped out of it.

Brave, brave Veronica.

She held the edges of her damp towel, her dignity not damaged in the least, and gazed up at him. "It's no good, Raj," she said. "We could fall into bed together now, but you'd still walk out in the end. I'm not putting myself through that again."

"I do want you," he said in despair. "I want to be with you." He shoved a hand through his hair, blew out a harsh breath. He felt tight inside, coiled, as if he had to do something or explode.

Maybe they could work it out. He could try. For her, he would try.

"I'll come to Aliz when I can. You'll be traveling, too—we'll meet in different places, take it a day at a time."

She shook her head sadly. Her hair was starting to dry, curling over her shoulders and down her back. She was as wild and untamed as Goa, as beautiful as the sea. He wanted to possess her, ached to possess her.

Frustration arced through him. He knew she wasn't going to accept what he was trying to offer. What was he offering, really?

"It's not enough, Raj," she said. "I want more. I'm not going to settle for half a life with you."

"It's all I can give you," he said, aching for her. He wanted to give her exactly what she desired. But he was afraid he would fail if he tried to take it that far. He had to start small.

She smiled sadly. "I know. But it's not enough for me. Some women might accept whatever sort of life they could get with the man they love, but I won't. I can't. I've already lost something precious to me, and survived the experience. I'll survive you, too."

Love? She loved him?

He was stunned into silence. He couldn't think of a thing to say. He didn't need to.

She did it for him.

"Goodbye, Raj."

The days turned into a week, and then two weeks, three weeks, and still the pain of losing Raj was as raw as it had been that day in her bedroom when he'd held her close and tried to give her what he thought she wanted.

It still made her angry. And so very frustrated.

Veronica steepled her hands on her desk and rested her chin on the point. She'd been busy these past weeks. She'd worked hard to see her vision for Aliz come to fruition. There'd been endless meetings, phone calls, interviews and a speech to the nation.

Aliz wasn't out of the woods yet, but things were looking better. The economy was stabilizing, and foreign investment was beginning to trickle in again. People were getting fed and things were getting built.

She couldn't ask for more.

Her gaze strayed to the evergreen garland decked with red and gold ribbon that draped over the fireplace in her office. It was almost Christmas, but she hadn't taken time to do anything to prepare. There was no one to shop for, no one to bake cookies for, no one to sit before the tree and enjoy the lights with. She wouldn't even have a tree if it weren't for the fact she had a housekeeping staff who had put one up for her because they'd always put one up for the Bruns.

It stood in her residence, decorated with silver and red and gold, the white lights always on whenever she walked in at the end of the day. There were no presents beneath it. She thought of her baby with a pang. He would have been almost eight months old. He wouldn't have understood what the glitter and presents were about, but he would have likely relished the bright colors and enjoyed tearing the paper.

Veronica didn't bother trying to sniff back the tears that happened whenever she thought of moments like this. It hurt, but she no longer felt as if she was solely responsible for her loss.

She had Raj to thank for that.

Her private cell phone rang and she jumped. It was not Raj's name on the display. She hadn't expected it would be, yet she always seemed to hope it might. But why? There was nothing but heartache in going down that road.

And she'd had enough heartache to last a lifetime.

"Hello, Brady," she said as she answered the call.

"Angel," he replied. "How are you? It's been a few days and I wanted to check."

"I'm fine," she said, resting her forehead in one hand. "How about you? Any celebrity gossip for me?"

Brady chuckled. "I've heard some juicy things about a certain new heartthrob and a Hollywood icon," he said. Then he spent the next fifteen minutes giving her every salacious detail of a May-December affair currently delighting the Rodeo Drive set.

"So what are you doing for Christmas?" he asked when he'd finished the tale.

"Nothing much. I have a country to run, in case you hadn't noticed."

"Surely you can spare a few hours for fun. Come to the Hotel Lefevre tomorrow night. I'm throwing a party."

Veronica blinked. "The Hotel Lefevre? In Aliz City?" It was the oldest and best hotel on the island. Understated and elegant, it had suffered through the economic crisis like everywhere else. That it was still open was a miracle, though the owners had had to sell off many of the treasured paintings that had once adorned the walls, including one that van Gogh had painted for the original owners when he'd spent time on the island before going to France.

"Yes. I've decided I want to go somewhere nice, and I want my friends to come, too. Aliz is a charming island. I hear it's making a come-back."

Her heart swelled with gratitude and love for her friend. "Brady, I…" She didn't know what to say. "Are you here now?"

"We just arrived this morning."

"We?"

"Me and Susan. I really want you to meet her."

"Susan?" She was beginning to feel like a parrot.

Brady sighed. "The woman I plan to spend the rest of my life with."

Veronica's mouth dropped open. "Brady, when I saw you in London, there was no one in your life. What happened? And why didn't you tell me this first? It's the most important thing you've said so far!"

"It's crazy," he said, his voice filled with laughter. "I know that. But sometimes you just know when you've found that special person."

A twinge of pain throbbed in her heart, but she listened delightedly as Brady talked about Susan—who wasn't an actress or a celebrity or a gold-digging wannabe who worked as a cock-tail waitress while waiting for her big break. No, Susan was a veterinarian he'd met when they'd both stopped to help an injured dog on the freeway.

"So will you come?" he finally said.

"Of course I'll come! I wouldn't miss this for anything."

She got off the phone feeling happier than she had in weeks. So her own life was a mess, but her friend was happy and he'd come all this way to show his support for her and her country. On Christmas.

Her eyes filled with tears again, but they were happy tears. Though seeing Brady would make her think of Raj, she would survive it. Besides, how could she be upset about being loved and wanted by her friends?

The next day was Christmas Eve. Veronica didn't have to work, but she went into her office and made some calls anyway. She'd already given her staff the day off, so the administrative wing was mostly silent. Afterward, she spent most of the day watching Christmas movies on television, then prepared for Brady's party. He'd sent over a formal invitation, and she knew there would be television cameras when she arrived.

It was part of the process, something that would delight people, and she dressed with care for the appearance. She donned a long red dress, strapless, that shimmered as she walked. The fabric was iridescent, gathered at the waist, and fell into a full skirt that was given shape by a tulle slip beneath. She wrapped a silver shawl around her shoulders and carried a small silver clutch. Silver-jeweled strappy high heels rounded out the look.

A bodyguard in a tuxedo opened the limo door for her as she emerged from her private entrance. He was Alizean, tall and handsome, but there was no spark of desire as she gazed at him in his black coat and tie. He climbed in beside her and they were on their way.

The media was camped out in front of the Hotel Lefrevre, and Veronica did her best to look glamorous and happy. She waved as the cameras flashed, then turned and posed—an old habit—before entering the hotel. Brady was waiting for her, a petite, smiling woman at his side. Veronica hugged them both as Brady introduced Susan. She was truly happy for them, and yet she was jealous, too.

If only her own love life had gone so smoothly. But Susan was a delightful woman, and Veronica found that she really liked talking with Brady's new love. Susan was down-to-earth, no-nonsense. She was pretty, but not gorgeous in that fake way that Hollywood encouraged.

They moved toward the old ballroom, and Veronica stopped in the entry, her head tilting back as she took it all in. The grand room was decorated beautifully, with candles, greenery and shiny lights and bows reflecting from the mirrored surfaces along the walls. The plaster was chipped in places, the paint faded, but it wouldn't remain that way for long if they had many more parties like this one. The room was filled with food and people, and Veronica's heart felt full.

"Thank you, Brady," she said, squeezing his arm when he came over and handed her a glass of champagne.

"For what?"

"For this. For doing this here. It means so much."

He smiled back, his gaze flickering to a point over her shoulder before coming to rest on her face again. "You might not thank me when you see what I've brought along with me."

She looked at her friend for a full moment— and then the hairs on her neck prickled as if an electrical current had zapped through the air. She knew who she would see the moment she turned.

He was, as always, achingly handsome. Her heart twisted in her chest. Looking at him hurt. And it made her happy, too.

"Damn it, Brady," she said to the man at her side. "You're always interfering."

He shrugged. "It's my nature." Then he kissed her on the cheek. "Don't say I never gave you anything."

She started to tell him he was an ass, but he'd disappeared. Raj smiled at her, and her insides melted. She had to work hard to keep the frown on her face.

"Hello, Veronica."

"Why are you here?"

His laugh was so rich, so beautiful to her ears. God, she'd missed him. And she didn't want to do this. Because she would have to miss him again when it was over.

"I've missed that directness of yours," he said. "You have no idea how refreshing it can be."

Her heart was thundering. "If you're about to tell me how other women are just not a challenge after me, save your breath. I don't want to hear it."

He looked puzzled. "I wasn't planning to say anything of the sort."

Looking at him made her ache. It brought all the loneliness of her life crashing down on her. "I really don't want to stand here and talk to you like everything is normal, Raj, so you'll have to excuse me."

She had to escape, right now, before she fell apart in front of everyone. Before she ranted and railed and told him what a miserable bastard he was for not loving her back. Before she revealed how pitiful she was because she still loved him, and a part of her was almost willing to take whatever crumbs he might bestow if only she could have another night, another day, another moment in time where they laughed and talked and made love as if they cared about each other.

Blindly, she turned and fled. When she reached the hall, she hesitated only a moment before she headed for the ladies' room, shoving open the door and going over to the small sink to press her hands on either side and breathe. Her face in the mirror looked perfectly normal, but she didn't feel normal.

The door swung open again and then Raj was there, looming in the mirror behind her. She heard the twist of the lock in the door and she spun to face him.

"Get out."

"It's like déjà vu," he said, his sensual mouth curving into a smile. "You, me, a ladies' room."

It was a much smaller ladies' room, with only this sink and mirror, the delicately papered walls and another door that led into the single toilet. There was no space, and she couldn't breathe with him so close. He filled her senses, made her ache with longing.

"It's a nightmare," she said. "I had no idea you hated me so much."

His brows drew together, two hard slashes over his golden eyes. "Hate you? My God, Veronica, I'm here because I can't forget you. Because I need you. Hate is the furthest thing from my mind."

She swallowed, shook her head, prayed the tears wouldn't fall. Because it was Christmas Eve and she was feeling vulnerable. Because she missed her baby, missed him. Because she was alone in this world and feeling very, very sorry for herself right now.

"Need isn't enough, is it? I need food to live, but I don't need chocolate cake. You need sex, but it doesn't have to be me."

He was beginning to look angry. "Sex? You think I'm here for sex?"

"What else? You've already told me it can be nothing more."

He blew out a breath. "I was wrong." Because he'd tried to move on with his life, tried to forget about the few days he'd shared with Veronica, the days where he'd felt more alive than he ever had before. He'd gone back to London, and then on to New York. When New York didn't work, when he still felt so restless he wanted to howl, he'd gone to Los Angeles.

In the past, when he wanted to escape, when he wanted peace, he'd gone to the house in Goa. But he couldn't go there anymore. Because he couldn't imagine himself there without her.

"You've ruined it for me," he said, watching the way her lip trembled so slightly, the way she was determined not to break in front of him.

She was so strong, so beautiful. She took his breath away. And he'd realized during the long, lonely few weeks without her that he didn't want to live like that anymore. He'd been denying himself because he'd thought he was doing the best thing for her. But the truth was that he'd been cheating them both.

"Ruined what?" she asked.

"Being alone."

She sucked in a breath, hugged her arms around herself. Bit her lip. An arrow of pure lust shot through him. That was *his* lip to bite.

"I'm the President of Aliz," she said softly. "I have a two-year term. This is my home. I can't go with you to Goa, or to London, just to keep you from being lonely. Nor do I want to."

"Do you still love me?" he said, his heart careening in his chest. He didn't think she'd stopped in three weeks time, but he wouldn't put anything past Veronica St. Germaine. The woman was a force to be reckoned with. If she wanted to stop loving him, she could. She was a woman who didn't shrink from challenges.

She turned her head away, but he could still see her face in the mirror. Two red spots bloomed on her cheeks. Her nostrils flared. Her mouth was a flat line as she compressed her lips. "Does it matter?" she finally said.

"It matters to me."

Her head snapped around, her eyes flashing angrily. "Why? So you can congratulate yourself yet again on your amazing skills?"

"Skills?"

"Those in which you deny yourself any chance at happiness simply to prove what a strong man you are."

He'd hurt her deeply, more deeply than he'd realized. And he wasn't proud of himself for it. "I have no wish to deny anything." He clenched his fists as his side, frustration hammering through him. "I'm here because I can't deny it."

She lifted her chin. "I need more from you, Raj. Telling me you want me isn't enough."

He swore. "I know." And then he resolved to lay it all out there. If she rejected him, it was nothing less than he deserved. But he had to take the chance. "I love you, Veronica. I can't live without you. I don't want to."

She slumped against the sink, her red dress

shimmering in the low light of the small room. "Did you just say…?"

He closed the distance between them, gripped her shoulders and put a finger under her chin. Lifted it so she had to look at him. Her eyes were liquid, beautiful blue pools in which he wanted to drown.

"I've spent my life running away, because it's all I knew. Because my mother was a drug addict and we were homeless more than we weren't. Because my father let us go and never bothered to find us again. Running is what I know, Veronica. Staying is much harder." He sucked in a breath. It felt like razor blades in his throat. "I'm afraid of unpacking the suitcase. Afraid that I'll have to move again tomorrow. Much easier to stay in motion. But you're in Aliz, and my heart is with you. You're the strongest, bravest person I know. I can't imagine my life without you in it. *You* are my home."

She gripped his sleeves then, her fingers twisting into the fabric. "I'm mad at you," she said, though her eyes were shining. "I really should make you sweat it out. I should make you wonder if you've ruined this irreparably."

"Have I?"

She gave her head a tiny shake, and then he was kissing her with all the pent-up passion and love that he could no longer deny. That he no longer wanted to deny. Her arms slipped around his neck, her body melding to his as if it had been made to do so.

"I love you, Raj," she said when he finally let her breathe again. "But I'm still mad at you."

He laughed against her throat, his lips nuzzling the sweet skin of her neck. "I'll look forward to letting you take your revenge against me. I'll even let you tie me up if it pleases you."

"Don't tempt me."

Veronica awoke sleepily, the church bells in the Aliz City cathedral chiming 4:00 a.m. on Christmas Day. It was still dark out, and her body was languid, lazy. She stretched, a pleasurable ache between her thighs. The bed was empty except for her. She sat up, smiling at the long length of her robe sash that was still knotted to one bedpost. She'd tied him up all right. Tied him up and tortured him until he'd begged her to put him out of his misery.

Until she'd taken him in her mouth and sent him to heaven.

Oh, yes, she'd gotten her revenge. A very pleasurable revenge indeed.

She slipped from the bed and found her robe. It took her a minute to untie the sash, but she did, slipping it around her waist and knotting it loosely. Then she went in search of Raj, knowing instinctively that he hadn't left her in the night.

She found him in the living room, sitting on the couch in the glow of the tree. He looked up when she approached, smiled that sexy smile she loved so much.

"I don't think I've ever sat and just watched the lights before," he said.

She knew he'd never really had an opportunity to do so in the past, and her heart hurt for the little boy he'd been. Moving from shelter to shelter and home to home. She sank beside him and curled up against his warm body. He slipped an arm around her.

"I'm sorry I didn't get you anything," she said, mesmerized by the twinkling lights. "But I didn't know you'd be here."

He laughed softly. "You gave me all I wanted," he said. Then he kissed the top of her head. A small package appeared in front of her nose.

"What's this?"

"I came prepared."

"Now I really feel bad," she said.

"Don't."

She sighed and untied the gold ribbon. Inside the red box was another box, nestled in tissue paper. A velvet box.

Her gaze flew to his. "Earrings," she said. "You've bought me earrings. I'll always treasure them."

He laughed. "Open it, Veronica. Stop guessing."

She did, her heart in her throat. It wasn't a pair of earrings. Her eyes filled until the large, emerald-cut diamond surrounded by smaller diamonds was nothing more than a blur.

"You can say no," he said. "I'd understand. Or you can say yes, and we'll have a long engagement."

She arched an eyebrow, sniffling. "Is the long engagement a condition?"

"No. I'm simply trying to give you a way out."

She shook her head. "I knew you were far too pretty to be smart. Men can't be gorgeous and brainy at the same time, you know."

She felt the tension coiling in his body. "Are you saying yes?"

A single tear spilled down her cheek. "Is this what you really want?"

"Do you think I'd ask if it weren't?"

"You didn't ask," she pointed out.

He smiled, and her heart squeezed with love. Then he slipped from the couch and got onto one knee. "I'm doing this right," he said, "because I don't ever want you to believe I didn't want this. Veronica, will you marry me?"

Her heart filled to bursting. Home. This was home—this moment, this feeling. This man. "Yes," she said simply.

Raj slipped the ring onto her finger. And then he made love to her on the Persian carpet in front of the Christmas tree.

There would never be, with the exception of their third child born on December 25 a few years hence, a more perfect gift than the one they shared on this particular Christmas.

* * * * *